Charla

CW00803023

Also published by New Guild

The Shield of Mashona
Rainy Days and Mondays
A Child of Silence
Elvis in Wonderland
S.O.S. - Men Against the Sea
Privy to the Mayor's Council
(a two-story anthology)
Melody for Lizzie

For Jacky with much love

Charlatan

Gary Orchard

NEW
GUILD

A New Guild Book

Published by New Era Writer's Guild (UK) Ltd
5 Cogdean Walk, Corfe Mullen
Wimborne Minster, Dorset BH21 3XB

PO Box 11476
Bloubergrant 7443, South Africa
Tel: (+21) 557 6281
Fax (+21) 557 0704

PO Box 100-806
North Shore Mail Centre
Auckland 10, New Zealand
Tel/fax: (+9) 443 8069

British Library Cataloguing in Publication Data. A catalogue record for
this book is available from the British Libary

ISBN 1 899694 20 X

This book was designed and produced by
Crispin Goodall Design Ltd
463 Ashley Road
Poole, Dorset BH14 OAX

Printed the United Kingdom by Warwick Printing Company Ltd

Chapter 1

Billy always wore the strap of his bass guitar over one shoulder. It was a good image. The hard rocker, shooting from the hip.

That wasn't why he did it, though.

He did it so that he could throw the damn thing away if anything went wrong with the power.

When he was seven, Billy had stuck his fingers into a mains socket to see what would happen. Once he had found out, he had swapped inquisitiveness for extreme caution.

Molly laughed at him for it, but Billy didn't care. She didn't have to wear a potentially lethal weapon around her neck. In fact, Molly wore very little. Just a pair of red high heels, a G-string and a pair of tassels.

Billy watched the tassels rotate in opposite directions.

'And for this,' he mused, 'I gave up an audition with the London Philharmonic!'

Standing by the side of the stage, Mike Menagerie was sweating. He took a swig from the hip-flask he always carried, and winced. Warm brown ale from a hip-flask still tasted disgusting, but the malt whisky days were still a long way off.

A sudden roar went up from the crowd. Mike blinked. At first he couldn't tell what had caused the outburst. Then he saw Molly stagger back from the front of the stage clutching her chest.

His first thought was that she'd been hurt, perhaps punched or stabbed. Then he saw the greaser in the front row waving something above his head. So, she'd only lost a tassel after all.

The band went into the middle eight for a second time. Molly made a break for the wings. The look in her eyes meant she was mad as hell. Above the sound of the band a chant went up.

'Get 'em off, get 'em off!'

At this point Mike couldn't tell if they were referring to the band or the rest of Molly's scanty attire. Either one spelled disaster. The Hell-fire Club is a bad place to bomb, and this evening was shaping up to be a regular Hiroshima.

Molly barged past, elbowing Mike out of the way as she did so. Mike grabbed her arm and spun her around.

'Where the fuck do you think you're going?' he demanded.

'Did you see what that animal did to me?' Molly shot back. 'Nearly pulled my bloody nipple off!'

'So what?'

'So it bloody hurt, that's so what!'

The chant from the crowd was growing louder. Mike glanced at the stage. Billy and Frank had retreated back to the drum kit and were casting nervous glances left and right, trying to figure out the quickest exit. Davy was playing drums from a half-standing position, ready to run.

The crowd pushed forward, like some mythical sea monster, complete with tentacles, ready to snare anyone foolish enough to stray within reach. The three remaining members of Lookalike had no intention of getting anywhere near that close, but they were running out of room.

Mike ground his teeth and swore. He turned back to Molly.

'Get back out there, you stupid bitch, or none of us are going to get out of here in one piece!'

'They want me to take my clothes off!'

Mike could not believe his ears. 'So friggin' what? You haven't got that many left anyway.'

Molly folded her arms over her sweating breasts. 'I'm not a stripper,' she declared.

'You were when I found you,' Mike retorted.

She had been, too, and a very good one at that. Working under the name of Norma Jean, she had exploited a passing resemblance to Marilyn Monroe for all it was worth. With the right dress, make-up and hair the likeness was really quite striking and the punters lapped it up.

Not much of the illusion remained now. The make-up was smeared, her hair hung in rat-tails and her clothes had been discarded long ago. Now she looked like any other sweaty, near-nude, overweight blonde. But she might mean the difference between walking home in one piece or being driven away in an ambulance.

'You said I wouldn't have to strip any more,' she whined. 'Not completely anyway. I don't mind the tassels. That's artistic, not everyone can do that, but I'm not stripping, no way!'

Someone threw a bottle onto the stage. It exploded in almost perfect time with a cymbal smash. Mike glanced towards the noise and the absurdity of the situation struck him so hard he felt dizzy.

The remaining band members, dressed up as the Marx Brothers, were attempting to hold back hostile hordes of Hell's Angels with a wall of sound. While he discussed the artistic merits of tassel-twirling with a near-naked Monroe clone!

'Keep playing, you bastards!' he shouted. 'If you stop playing we're all dead!'

As he turned back, a bouncer called Cyril clapped a hand the size of a small country onto his shoulder.

'Mr Brass suggests,' said Cyril politely, 'that the bimbo,' he jerked a thumb towards Molly, 'gets back on stage, gets 'em off and stays there, until Mr Brass gives the okay to do otherwise.'

Mike spread his hands in his best 'it's nothing to do with me' gesture. Molly scowled and stayed put. Cyril's grip tightened and Mike felt his knees start to give way.

'Please,' he whimpered.

Molly jabbed him in the chest hard enough to puncture a lung.

'If you were a proper manager,' she screamed at him, 'we wouldn't have to play places like this.'

'Never again,' Mike hissed through clenched teeth. 'I swear, never again. Just, please, get back out there.'

Molly grunted and kicked off her red shoes.

'This is the last bloody time,' she shouted, and launched herself back on stage. A raucous cheer greeted her entrance.

'Very good,' said Cyril smoothly. 'Now, let's go and have a little talk with Mr Brass about whether he's still going to pay you, or just let you keep your balls.'

Chapter 2

There are rats in those garages.

Big ones, with red, darting eyes. They live in the rotting carcasses of the cars that were left behind when the tenants moved out.

North Street is a dead street now. Condemned long ago. No one comes here any more, not for any legitimate purpose anyway. Windows are smashed or boarded up. Houses are left to fall apart in their own good time. The evolution of decay.

The street has an evil reputation. Murders have been committed here. Bodies hidden, some yet to be found, so they say. Virgins deflowered. Dope deals struck and reneged on. Old scores settled.

Evil.

The last functional street lamp is way back at the junction with Coast Road. Clouds cover the moon. Anything could be hiding in those shadows. And it is cold.

Sally Parker wasn't dressed for the cold. Hardly dressed at all by polite standards. She sported a short denim jacket, worn open to show off the merchandise. Beneath that, a red halter top, two sizes too small, clung to the contours of her body like a second skin and left her midriff bare. A black miniskirt that barely reached her thighs, black stockings and black high heels completed her outfit. Her hair was a peroxide tangle proclaiming that if you wanted more fun with this particular blonde you could expect to pay accordingly. There was nothing subtle about the way she looked or the way she walked. In all of Sally's twenty-two years' experience on this planet the one lesson she had learnt above all was that it pays to advertise.

She stopped at the short alleyway leading to the garages, the echo of her high heels fading away on the cold night air. There are rats in those garages, she thought. Big ones. Guarding their concrete caves as jealously as any fabled dragon. Sally shrugged and moved forward.

It was even darker back here than on the street. Shadow lay upon shadow, making everything strange and distorted. In the far corner, a lumpier piece of darkness suggested the shape of a car. Sally stepped towards it. Headlights came on, pinning her in their glare, blinding her. She swore. The headlights went out. Sally blinked away the spots before her eyes. She heard a car door open. The car's interior light went on. The driver stepped out and stood by the open door. She could make out another figure in the passenger seat, indistinct, huddled in the folds of an over-large anorak. The driver grinned, his breath emerging as a tiny white cloud of fetid breath. His name was Sammy Pierce.

He stood a little over six feet tall and had bad skin, a paunch and lank, greasy hair to go with the bad breath. He'd never been able to afford her. Until now. Now he had something to barter with. When he'd first approached her in the pub, the smell of best bitter fighting for supremacy with the B.O., she'd thought he was lying. She knew that he worked at the Big House all right, that much was true. Nobody really knew what went on up there, so people made things up. By now it had gained almost as bad a reputation as North Street.

It had been the photographs that had finally convinced her to take the chance. Blurred and out of focus they may have been, but clear enough to spark her interest, make her take the risk. If it was true, the price would be high. Giving herself to Sammy Pierce was not well up on her agenda of things she most wanted to do. Still, she reasoned, I've had worse, and if he's lying, well, the flick-knife in her coat pocket had scared off better men than he could ever dream of being.

Sammy leant an arm on the car's roof. 'Sorry about that,' he said. 'I wanted to be sure it was you. You're late.'

Sally shrugged. 'I'm worth waiting for.'

Sammy licked his lips. 'That you are,' he agreed, 'that you are.' He leant back inside the car. 'Come on out and say hello to our guest, Dave,' he said. At first the figure in the passenger seat didn't move. Then slowly he opened the door and got out. He was shorter than Sammy, thinner; even in deep shadow his face looked thin and pinched. 'Hello,' he said.

'Charmed,' Sally responded. For a few seconds all three stood looking at each other. 'Well?' said Sally. 'Shall we get on with it, or do you expect me to stand here all night freezing my tits off?'

Sammy laughed. 'Can't have that, can we? Just need to take a few precautions, though. You do believe in taking precautions, don't you, love?'

Sally gave him a look.

Sammy gave a small embarrassed cough. 'Yea, 'course you do,' he muttered. 'Follow me.' He moved to the back of the car. Sally followed, Dave came up on the other side. 'I've told you about the security problems, haven't I?' Sammy continued.

Sally nodded. 'So?'

'Well, we can't just drive in there with you in the back seat, you'd be stopped. So . . . we have to smuggle you in.'

Sally frowned. Light was beginning to dawn and she didn't like what it showed. 'What do you mean?' she asked.

Sammy grinned and opened the boot.

'Get in,' he said.

Chapter 3

Denby Lodge.

Everybody called it the Big House. It was as ugly as sin. An architectural mongrel with a sway-backed roof, an ivy-choked façade and a pair of crumbling stone lions to guard the main entrance. An annexe, all white paint and steel window frames, had been attached to the west side of the house like a strange organ transplant that the body of the house had rejected.

Not that it mattered much. Few people ever saw the Big House these days. Sitting in two acres of grounds, surrounded by trees and a high brick wall, it kept itself to itself. Those with long memories could remember it being a country retreat for some distant relative of royalty and, very briefly, a private school. For many years the house was empty and forgotten. Then, in the late 1950s, a fleet of unmarked vans arrived and a small army of workmen began extensive renovations.

From that day to this no one ever really found out what went on at the Big House. Over-active imaginations pondered long and pontificated loudly, but no one ever really knew. The few local people who were employed there became strangely tight-lipped. Adventurous youths who scaled the walls on a dare, or intent on some petty larceny, soon found themselves confronted by large, dark-uniformed men and salivating German shepherd dogs. No charges were ever pressed, but repeat offenders were unheard of. In this way the Big House had acquired a mysterious and fearful reputation.

In the main reception area of the Denby Lodge annexe sat an automated console containing video monitors, telephones, a switchboard and various emergency buttons. Sammy Pierce called it Mission Control. It looked hi-tech and sophisticated, but then, Sammy thought a transistor radio was hi-tech as long as it had enough buttons to press and knobs to twiddle.

The reception was dimly lit to save on energy. Brown leather chairs and withered pot plants struggled to give it an air of commercialism, but no one was fooled. The public never set foot in this place. No sales rep ever rested his briefcase on the scratched coffee-table or stubbed out his cigarette in the roots of a dying aspidistra. Visitors were few. Those who did arrive were ushered quickly through the double doors behind the desk and whisked away into the sterile heart of the Big House.

Now Sammy Pierce sat in what he always regarded as the seat of power behind the Mission Control desk. Dave Sadler stood nervously to one side, chewing on a ragged fingernail. Sally Parker stood centre stage and pulled the halter top away from her body.

'You'll have to pay for this,' she threatened. 'Just look at it.' Sammy looked and felt sweat break out on his upper lip. A greasy mark was smeared across the crimson material. More of the same was smudged across Sally's cheeks and forehead.

'And these.' Sally pointed to her stockings, now torn through at the knees.

'Okay, okay,' Sammy muttered. 'It's no big deal.'

'No big deal!' Sally rounded on him. 'You try being shut up in a bloody car boot for half an hour and see how you like it!'

'Calm down, calm down.' Sammy made placating gestures with his hands. 'I'll pay for them, all right?'

'You'd bloody well better!'

Sally stopped grumbling about her indignities and took in her surroundings for the first time.

'What is this place, anyway?' she asked.

Sammy grinned at her. 'They call it a Genetic Research Facility.' He leaned closer and leered at her in the half-light. 'But you can call it Heaven.'

Sally snorted. 'So far I call it bullshit.'

'You'll change your mind. Did you bring the photo?'

'Yeah.' Sally dug into her jacket pocket and pulled out a piece of folded paper. 'Here it is.'

Sammy took it from her and unfolded it. It was a picture clipped from a magazine. It showed Rod Stewart in his days with The Faces, all tartan scarf and hair like he'd just been plugged into the mains. Sammy nodded. 'It'll do.'

'So what happens now?'

'Simple. I set up the equipment, we fetch the guest of honour and the party can begin.'

Sally pouted. 'In that case I'd better go and get cleaned up. Don't want to meet the man of my dreams looking like something the cat dragged in, do I?' She didn't wait for a reply, just turned on her heel and marched through the door marked 'Ladies'.

Sammy fumed as he watched the door slam behind her.

'Why did God have to make all the good-looking ones so bloody mouthy?' he asked of no one in particular. 'And you were no bloody help!' He almost shouted the words and Dave jumped, tearing his jagged fingernail painfully.

'What was I supposed to do?' he whined.

'Nothing. You just sit back and let me do all the work, as usual.' Sammy turned away, back towards the console and its comforting array of knobs and switches. Cool it, he told himself, don't let your nerves get the better of you. He flicked one of the switches and a video screen came to life. The camera which fed the picture to the screen was high up and gave a wide-angle view of a cell-like room. A sink, a toilet and a narrow cot were the room's only furnishings. A figure lay on the cot, huddled under a single blanket. Occasionally the figure would move, as if disturbed by a dream. Sammy rubbed his hands, a miser gloating over his hoard of treasure.

'Not long now, sunshine,' he whispered, 'not long at all.'

Charlie had once read a book called *The Diary of Anne Frank*. That was in the days when they used to give him lots to read. A whole library of stuff: fiction, biographies, children's books, comics. Charlie had liked that. The stories made pretty pictures in his head. His memory had been good, too. They always tested him on what he had read, and he always got it right.

Charlie enjoyed getting things right. They would smile and tell him how clever he was. He enjoyed making them happy.

Nowadays they never gave him books to read. They said they'd progressed beyond that point. Now they just showed him pictures on a TV screen. Not ordinary pictures, though. Oh no. Charlie liked regular TV. He would watch as much TV as he could. This was not regular TV. These pictures made him feel strange. Made him do the sexy thing. Charlie knew it was wrong, but he couldn't help himself.

At least it was better than doing the other thing. The thing he would not let himself even think about. Charlie wasn't stupid. He knew they only got him to do the sexy thing to keep him occupied until they wanted him to do the other thing again.

It was then that he remembered Anne Frank. That story had been so sad, and yet so brave. An entire family hiding from the German soldiers in a secret room. They stayed there for a long time, safe and secure.

That's what Charlie needed: a secret room to hide in. But where could he go? He had no house he could go to and lock himself in, no attic to hide in.

Still, a room doesn't have to be made of four walls and a roof, does it? Of course not, he told himself. A room is what you make it. So Charlie made his own room. Right inside his head. A room that no one else knew about, where no one could find him.

Of course, the Germans eventually found Anne Frank, but Charlie tried not to think about that. Nor was it German soldiers who were looking for him. It was the Bad Man. Charlie didn't know his name, but that was how he always thought of him, with capitals. The Bad Man.

Charlie didn't know he was bad when they first met. He was nice then.

'Do you play chess?' the Bad Man had asked. When Charlie said no, he offered to teach him. At first it had been fun, the black and white squares, the elegant carved pieces. Then something had changed. Charlie didn't know what or how, but the pieces suddenly became red and sticky and before he knew it he was doing the other thing. The thing he didn't dare think about.

He could still see the Bad Man's eyes. Bright red they were, the type of eyes that glowed in the dark. Just like Bela Lugosi in those old Dracula movies. Charlie had read somewhere that they had shone a light in Bela's eyes to make them look like that. The Bad Man didn't need any light; his eyes glowed from within.

For days now (or was it weeks?), the Bad Man had been looking for him. Rampaging through Charlie's psychic house, kicking down doors. He hadn't found him yet, Charlie's secret room was too well hidden, but boy, had he come close! This last time was the closest of all. So close Charlie could hear him breathing, feel those red eyes burning him.

Charlie had wanted to cry out, to scream and to run, but he knew that would do no good. That would only tell the Bad Man where he was. So Charlie had kept very quiet and very still and eventually the Bad Man had gone away. And now Charlie was tired, so very, very tired, and all he wanted to do was sleep.

Sally Parker had a deep distrust of public lavatories. It all stemmed from the time she was sixteen and new to the game and not as streetwise as she was now. She'd been badly beaten up in the ladies' room of the Red Bull by what seemed at the time to be a female wrestler. In fact it had been a disgruntled housewife who had taken exception to the rather blatant advances Sally had been making towards her husband. The beating had been bad enough to keep Sally at home for three days, until the worst of the swelling had gone down, but it had taught her a valuable lesson. Her technique had improved after that. It was about that time that Sally had started to carry a knife. Even so, it had left her with misgivings about public lavatories of all kinds.

Not that the Ladies' Washroom (that's what the sign had said on the door) at the Big House looked like any public lavatory that Sally had ever seen before. It looked more like an operating theatre. Gleaming steel and chrome fixtures, blinding white ceramic tiles on the floor and walls. Antiseptically clean. The glaring fluorescent lighting rebounded from the sterile walls and the gleaming mirrored tiles above the pristine washbasins aggravating the exhaust-fume headache that had settled behind Sally's eyes.

She crossed to the basin and looked at herself in the mirror. She groaned.

'If he thinks I'm riding in that bloody boot on the way back . . .' she told her reflection, leaving the hidden threat at the end of the sentence unspoken.

She bent down and peered at her stockings, torn through at the knees. She winced as she gently plucked the material away from her scraped and bleeding knees.

'Bloody hell!' she muttered.

She straightened up and gave her reflection a wry smile.

'Serves you right,' she told herself, 'for trusting a nutter like Sammy Pierce.'

She twisted the hot tap viciously. Steam rose from the needle-fine spray. Sally pushed the plug into place and began to undress.

'Are you sure it's safe, leaving her all alone?' Dave Sadler was a worried man. It showed on every line of his thin, pinched face, in the short, nervous steps he took, the way he constantly looked over his shoulder, jumping at shadows.

'She's not likely to go anywhere, is she?' Sammy was more than a little disappointed by Dave's attitude. He hadn't said a word all evening and now he had a bad case of verbal diarrhoea. 'Besides,' he continued, 'we'll only be gone a couple of minutes. Just long enough to get our guest of honour ready for the party.'

'Why does it take the two of us?'

Sammy sighed. 'I told you. Sometimes he gets a bit worked up. It's just a precaution.'

'You mean he might get violent? You didn't say anything about his being violent.'

'I'll get bloody violent in a minute if you don't stop whining!' Sammy took a deep breath and continued in a more reasonable voice. 'Look, he's not violent, but sometimes he can be a bit awkward, that's why I nicked this from the storeroom last time I was in there.'

From his inside pocket, Sammy produced a slim syringe, its needle hidden by a plastic cover. It contained a pale yellow liquid.

Dave eyed it nervously. 'What is it?' he asked.

'Custard, for all I know, but it makes Charlie-boy as gentle as a lamb. Now stop worrying.'

For a few seconds the silence was broken only by the sound of their echoing footsteps.

'Are you sure you know how to work all that stuff?' Dave asked eventually.

'Yes, I'm sure,' Sammy snapped back. 'I told you, when I was on the day shift I saw them do it a hundred times. It's as simple as using a video machine.'

There was a slight pause, before Dave said, 'I thought you said you

14

blew up your last video machine?'

Sammy glared at him, for once speechless.

They had come to a halt outside a pale green metal door. A plastic nameplate bore the single word, 'CHARLATAN'.

Sammy turned to the door and slid back the round inspection plate. Inside, the room was lit by a dull glow coming from a single bulb, hidden behind a wire grille in the room's high ceiling. The room was really a cell. Its lone occupant lay still, hidden by a single blanket.

Sammy grinned. 'What did I tell you?' he demanded. 'Sleeping like a baby.'

He produced a large brass ring containing keys. Carefully selecting one, he inserted it into the lock and opened the door.

Chapter 4

Big-time rock promoters do not live with their mothers.

Mike Menagerie lived with his mother.

It was a constant, nagging reminder of his failure. Just like the Hellfire Club had been a failure. Well, perhaps not a total failure. Getting out alive was certainly a plus, but not getting paid and having most of the band's gear smashed up did not constitute a roaring success in Mike's book.

He moved with exaggerated care. Letting himself in by the back door, he removed his shoes and deliberately kept the lights off so as not to disturb his mother. Moving cautiously forward he rammed his knee painfully against the leg of the kitchen table, sending it scuttling across the linoleum. Mike hopped on one foot, clutching his injured knee and biting his tongue to stop himself yelling in pain.

'Michael?' His mother's voice. 'Is that you?'

'No, it's Jack the sodding Ripper!' he hissed through clenched teeth. 'Yes, Mum,' he said out loud. 'It's me. Didn't want to disturb you. Go back to sleep.'

'I wasn't asleep. You know I always wait up for you. Come up and tell me what happened.'

Mike sighed and turned on the lights to save himself further injury. He plodded dismally upstairs. She won't approve, he told himself. She never does. Norman Bates had it easy compared to me!

Doreen Smith had become a mother late in life. Her husband had left as soon as his son was born. Mike had taken it as a personal insult. Doreen doted on her only child, but disapproved strongly of his chosen profession. And the fact that he had adopted a ridiculous surname.

'What's wrong with your real name?' she asked him. 'Mike Smith is a good, dependable name.'

'It's boring,' he told her. 'People will think I'm that prat on the telly!'

'At least he has a decent job and wears nice clothes,' she'd retorted. And so the argument would go on. Endlessly.

Mike poked his head around the door to his mother's room, trying not to breathe in case she smelt the beer on his breath.

Doreen sat up in bed, a pink bedjacket around her shoulders and curlers in her hair, a half-empty box of Milk Tray within easy reach. She was watching an old Bogart movie on a portable black-and-white TV.

'Well, don't stand there like a wet weekend,' she said. 'Come here and tell me what happened.'

She patted a space by her side and Mike grudgingly crossed the room and sat on the very edge of the mattress.

Doreen sniffed. 'You've been drinking,' she stated.

'I am twenty-seven, Mother,' Mike replied petulantly. 'Besides, it was a club. I had to have a couple.'

Doreen grunted her disapproval and sniffed again, pointedly.

'So?' she demanded. 'How did it go?'

'Not as well as we'd have liked,' Mike admitted. It was no good lying to his mother; she had a built-in polygraph.

Doreen sniffed, accusingly.

'I don't know why you bother,' she said. 'You could have a proper job with your Uncle Brian any time you like.'

'I don't want to be a butcher, Mum.'

'It pays well.'

'I'm a vegetarian!'

'You wouldn't have to eat it, just sell it!'

'We're committed now, Mum. We have a summer season all lined up. I can't let all those holidaymakers down, now can I?'

'And afterwards? What then?'

Mike sighed. He was really too weary for this.

'All right,' he gave in. 'If we don't get a break over the summer, I'll go and work for Uncle Brian.'

In some ways, he thought, it will be a blessed relief.

Chapter 5

Tommy Hancock had enough problems without Sammy Pierce swan-ning off home with a case of the snuffles.

Still, the poor sod had looked really rough when he drove through the check-out point. His face had been a pasty grey colour and his voice sounded like someone had sandpapered his tonsils.

There had been a flu epidemic going the rounds and the night shift was almost at half strength as it was. Now Tommy would have to do yet another round himself to check up on that prat Sadler. Well, one of the other lads could give Sadler a lift home, or else he could get the bus. Tommy had enough on his plate without running a bloody taxi service as well.

Tommy used his master key to unlock the glass doors to the recep-tion area. It was deserted.

'Sadler?' he called.

Only a faint echo of his own voice came back to him.

Must be doing his rounds, Tommy mused, as he pushed on through the double doors to the main part of the building.

It was the smell that hit him first.

It smelt like blocked drains, or rotting compost, and it was strong enough to make him heave.

'Bloody hell!' he muttered, and coughed, the steak and kidney pie he had had for tea returning to haunt the back of his throat.

'Sadler!' he called. 'What the hell are you up to?'

No reply.

And then he saw the stain on the floor.

In the half-light it was a darker shadow among many, oozing from under the solid metal door of one of the research laboratories. Tommy shook his head. Shadows don't ooze like that, he told himself. But if it wasn't a shadow, then what was it? A puddle maybe? Sadler's spilt something, he decided. He's been messing around in the lab and knocked something over, that's what it is.

A small, sadistic part of his brain whispered, 'You don't really believe that, do you?'

Tommy held his breath to block out the smell.

He stepped carefully around the dark discharge on the floor and pushed open the door.

The lights were on inside. Not all of them, but enough.

Enough to see the three sprawled bodies, the jagged gashes in throats and stomachs, the blue-grey intestines that spilled onto the floor like an upturned basket of snakes. And enough to see the blood that lapped around his shoes.

Tommy Hancock leaned over and vomited.

Chapter 6

'And how are you today, Alice?'

Alice Green smiled. Such a nice young man, she thought. Always asks after my health. 'I'm not too bad,' she replied. 'Touch of arthritis, but I shouldn't complain.'

'And your daughter, is she over her cold?'

So considerate, he's never even met June! 'Just about, which is just as well. With a young family to look after, you can't afford to be ill. I mean, Simon does his best, but his job takes him away from home such a lot.'

'I always think it's a great shame when family life has to suffer just to make ends meet.'

'I couldn't agree more, but young people today don't seem to mind. They just get used to it, I suppose.'

A woman queuing behind gave a meaningful cough. Alice frowned at her. Mr Payne just smiled.

'We seem to be holding up traffic,' he said. 'I'll just take these two and let you get on.'

Alice picked up the faded check shirt and the dog-eared paperback. She clucked her tongue thoughtfully. 'Do you know?' she observed, 'I think someone brought another shirt like this in only this morning. I haven't had time to unpack it yet, but I'm sure it's in better condition than this. I'll just go and check, shall I?'

She made to bustle away towards the small back room. Her customer put out his hand, such warm hands he had, and stopped her.

'Please,' he said, 'there's no need. I've really taken such a shine to this one. Let someone else benefit from the better shirt. After all, isn't that what charity shops are all about?'

Alice positively beamed. What a charming gesture! 'Well,' she responded, 'if you're sure?'

'Positive.'

Alice wrapped the items up, charged him less than one pound for both and watched him leave the shop with a small pang of regret.

'Such a nice man,' she confided to her next customer. 'Comes in almost every week and always buys something. Such a nice man.'

As he walked down the street, Payne held the book in his hands. He flicked through the pages, pausing here and there. He ran his fingers over the print as a blind man would do and smiled. Such a good book, so rich and fulfilling. He glanced at the title, and realised he held the book upside-down and back to front. It didn't matter.

The worn check shirt in the plastic bag held the promise of even greater pleasure. No, he would not like one in better condition, thank you very much. That, after all, would defeat the object.

'Did you know, there's a religious sect in India that never wears any clothes to show their disdain for material wealth?'

'Cobblers!' Bob Stevens rammed the heel of his hand down onto the horn. The resulting blare of noise scared three years' growth out of a dawdling pedestrian.

'The only reason they don't wear any clothes,' Stevens continued, 'is so they can get their leg over more often. Dirty little buggers. No wonder there's so many of them.'

Dave March leaned back in his seat and grinned. 'That wasn't a racist remark by any chance, was it?' he asked with as much innocence as he could muster.

Stevens glared at him. 'Cobblers!' he muttered.

It was a well-known fact that Stevens had been 'let go' by the Met because of his racist attitude. The final straw had been an incident with a suspected West Indian dope dealer, a rubber hose and a mysteriously locked room. The dealer had been as guilty as sin, but the resultant bruises on his face had persuaded Stevens' superiors to insist that he hand in his papers.

It was Dave March's personal opinion that Stevens was no more a racist than the next man. Stevens, he considered, hated everyone equally. Black, yellow, brown, men, women, children, gays, foreigners, football supporters, and people who had fluffy dice hanging from their rear view mirror. The list was endless.

It was precisely because of this anti-social attitude that he had been recruited for S1, a semi-official task force attached to the Ministry of Defence. S1 were the expendables, spoken of in hushed whispers and never acknowledged in public at all. Compared to S1 the SAS were positive attention seekers.

Officially, the MOD employed a small cadre of 'Research Officers' whose work required access to certain information and sufficient funds to cover the purchase of outside expertise. No one ever questioned too closely the type of expertise that was required.

Effectively then, Stevens and March, and every other S1 field operative were self-employed, acting as sub-contractors to a Senior Research Officer known affectionately as the 'Juggler'. It was the Juggler's task to make sure resources were available at short notice and minimal cost to cover any and every contingency. When the Juggler balanced the books, the figures owed more to creative writing than good accounting practice. Stevens and March, for example, received a monthly retainer for their expertise in 'urban tactical initiatives'.

Stevens more succinctly defined it as a 'putting the boot in allowance'. Crude but accurate. Stevens was the bluntest of blunt instruments, a stocky, shaven-headed individual with close-set piggy eyes and permanent stubble. March was smaller with dark wavy hair curling up at his collar, his plump cheeks giving him a misleading baby-face. He was softly spoken and smiled a lot, and it was only when you looked into his eyes that you realised the gentle exterior masked a core of solid ice. Of the two he was by far the most dangerous, a mercenary soldier who had had enough of war, but had never lost the killer instinct.

Stevens pushed the reliable but rusty Escort through an amber light at the last second and turned sharp left.

'What bloody street are we looking for, again?' he asked.

'That one,' March replied, 'the one you've just passed.'

Stevens swore and slammed on the brakes amid a chorus of car horns and shouted oaths. He executed a quick, illegal U-turn, ignoring oncoming traffic and obscene gestures alike. With a flourish he swerved into the street he was looking for and pulled into the kerb. March grinned.

'Did you enjoy that?' he asked.

Stevens grinned back. 'Yeah,' he replied, and got out of the car.

The house they wanted was midway down the street. It was a basement flat, the area outside littered with empty milk bottles and bags of rubbish. Stevens banged on the door. No answer. He knocked again, harder.

'Come on,' he muttered, 'where the hell are you?'

March leant against the wall, hands stuffed into the pockets of his jeans. 'Maybe he's not in,' he offered.

'He'd better bloody well be in,' snapped Stevens, 'after we've traipsed all the way over here. Why he can't be on the sodding phone like normal people is beyond me.'

'As so many things are, I'm sure.' The voice came from behind and above them. They both jumped, March reaching instinctively inside his jacket.

Payne leant on the railing above them, grinning. 'Please,' he said, 'no violence. I do so hate having to mop up bloodstains from my porch, don't you?'

'How long have you been standing there?' Stevens demanded.

Payne consulted his watch languidly. 'Oh, about five minutes.' He smiled. 'To what do I owe the honour of this visit?' he asked.

'Open up and we'll tell you,' March replied.

Payne sighed and descended the basement steps. 'All right,' he said, 'but you must excuse the state of the place. You just can't get good cleaning staff these days.'

The front door opened onto a corridor. At the far end another door stood half open, revealing a washbasin and the side of a bath. Two other doors opened off from the right-hand side of the passageway. Payne moved ahead of his visitors. The first door they passed was a kitchen. Stevens wrinkled his nose at the pile of unwashed dishes and scattered boxes and tins. 'Jesus!' he muttered, 'the place is a pigsty.'

Payne disappeared into the second doorway. Stevens and March followed, and then stopped dead in their tracks.

At first they thought the girl was dead. And then she blinked. Eyes so large and empty, they dominated a thin, elfin face. She lay on a mattress tossed into a corner. Naked, curled into a foetal position, her thumb stuck firmly into her mouth. Sweat covered her body and dripped onto the stained and ruptured mattress.

The room itself was a combination living room and bedroom. Broken-down armchairs, piles of clothes, bottles and dirty plates littered the floor.

Payne dropped his recent purchases onto the mattress, next to the girl, and turned to face his guests. 'I don't believe you've met Sonia, have you?' he said.

'Jesus H. Christ,' March muttered, disbelievingly.

Stevens' face turned the colour of beetroot. He looked from the girl to Payne and back again.

'Do you like her?' Payne whispered.

Stevens turned his eyes towards him, a rabbit mesmerised by a snake. March felt his stomach take an elevator lurch.

'Bob?' he whispered. His partner did not respond. March moved forward, his limbs heavy as though wading through water; a static hum like an open telephone line seemed to have taken up residence in his head. Stevens continued to stare. The grin on Payne's face widened; his whole body seemed to grow, to become the focal point of the room, all other details blurring.

What the hell is going on here? March asked himself silently. He reached out a leaden hand to grab Stevens' arm. Blue sparks of static electricity shot up his arm. He pulled back with a curse, but the contact seemed to break the spell. The room came back into normal focus. Stevens uttered a low moan; he was sweating and shaking, like a racehorse who's been ridden too long and too hard. He shook his head as if to clear a fog, and his eyes lit up with a savage spark. Without warning Stevens lunged forward, grabbed Payne by the lapels and slammed him against the wall. Stevens was screaming in inarticulate rage. Payne was laughing, a keening, lunatic sound.

March grabbed his partner around the shoulders and heaved. It took all his strength to pull them apart. Stevens shook himself free of March's grip, his breathing strained, tears wetting his cheeks.

'What the hell did you do to him?' March demanded.

'Me?' Payne replied. 'Did you see me "do" anything?'

March shook his head. 'You're wanted at Denby,' he shouted. 'We'll wait in the car.' He turned on his heel and guided his stricken colleague towards the door.

Left alone, Payne stood very still, breathing deeply, savouring the atmosphere, absorbing the vibrations from the recent confrontation. He shuddered and licked his lips, a connoisseur pleasantly surprised by a fine vintage. He turned towards the girl. She was alert now, sitting on her haunches, every muscle of her body strained to breaking point. Her skin was soaked in sweat, tiny whimpering noises escaping her lips. Her eyes rolled back until only the whites were showing.

'Did you enjoy that, too?' Payne cooed. He ran his hand down her body and she spasmed as if jolted by electricity. Payne withdrew his hand and her body sagged against the mattress. Her eyelids closed, only her shallow breathing bearing testimony to the fact that she still lived.

Payne tipped his head to one side, as though listening to a secret voice.

'Denby,' he mused. 'What could they possibly want with me at Denby?' And then he laughed, a short, barking sound.

'Charlatan,' he said.

Christina Laker.

Her friends called her Tina. Her subordinates called her Ma'am. Her superiors only called her when something dirty needed doing. She'd been the Juggler for the clandestine task force known as S1 for six years now. She was still only forty-three and the smart money said she was still on the way up.

Christina sat in the office of the Project Director at Denby House. The Director himself, Sir Reginald Meres, paced up and down in front of the second-storey picture window that gave him an uninterrupted view of the sweeping drive leading up to Denby House. He was a dapper little man with a bald head, a bristling moustache and an air force tie. At this moment he was not a happy soul. He glanced at his watch and tutted.

'Where the hell is he?' he asked of no one in particular.

Christina crossed her legs.

Sir Reginald wished she wouldn't do that. She had very long legs and the sort of unobtrusive good looks that some men found irresistible and others regarded as old maid material. Sir Reginald fell into the former group. He let his gaze linger on the expanse of exposed thigh a fraction longer than was polite and felt a hot flush creep into his face. If Christina noticed it she gave no sign.

'He'll be here,' she said. 'March radioed in over an hour ago to say they were on their way.'

'I don't like this,' Sir Reginald retorted, 'not one bit.'

'You don't have to like it.' Christina's voice was crisp, matter of fact. 'In a live situation,' she quoted, 'control passes to the relevant Chief of Operations. In this case, to me. All you have to worry about, Sir Reginald, is trying to explain why your screening process was so lax that it gave someone like Sammy Pierce sufficient clearance to engineer this fiasco in the first place.'

Sir Reginald blushed to the roots of his non-existent hair.

'I meant Payne.' He almost spat the words. 'Damn it, Tina, the man's a loose cannon. I've said so from the start. If Payne had done his job properly Pierce would never have been able to trigger the lethal response so easily.'

Christina's mouth hardened into a thin line, annoyed at the over-familiarity of being called Tina more than at the blustering of a man afraid of losing his job. She rose quickly from her chair and crossed to Sir Reginald, crowding him. She was half a head taller than he was; her ice-blue eyes stared down into his watery brown pools. Christina smiled sweetly.

'Payne is my responsibility,' she told him with charming ambiguity. 'Remember that.'

Standing this close he could smell her perfume, see each individual eyelash, trace the fine, almost invisible hairs along her upper lip, see the gentle swell of a pale breast between the buttons of her crisp white blouse.

'Oh God!' he thought, 'what I wouldn't give to spread you over this desk and wipe that smug look off your face!'

The sound of tyres on gravel interrupted his erotic musings. He turned to the window. From his vantage point he saw a rusty Escort come to a halt in front of the main doors. Stevens and March got out and, after a pause, Payne emerged from the back.

Meres grunted. 'Looks like a bloody scarecrow,' he muttered. Payne wore a shabby trench-coat, patched cords, a frayed and grubby green shirt and trainers that had seen better days. Meres craned forward, resting his head against the glass.

'Bloody man's got odd socks on!' he announced. He turned away from the window. 'Bloody little misfit wears odd socks. I swear he does it on purpose just to annoy me.'

'He does do it on purpose,' Christina replied coolly. 'But not just to annoy you. You know exactly why he does it. He wouldn't be half as effective if he didn't.'

Meres sighed. 'Why him?' he muttered. 'Of all the case officers we have, why did it have to be Payne?'

Christina smiled. 'Come on,' she said, 'let's get it over with.'

Payne was waiting in Reception when Meres and Christina emerged from the lift. He smiled broadly when he caught sight of them.

'Reggie!' he announced joyfully. 'Still wearing the tie, I see. Such a shame the RAF wouldn't take you. Or the Army. Flat feet or something, wasn't it? I know a nice little shop where you can pick up all sorts of second-hand service ties when that one wears out. Probably get you some medals to go with it; how does that sound?'

Meres made a spluttering, choking sound. Payne smiled and glanced at Christina. 'Why am I here?' he asked.

'Follow me,' she said, and moved off along the corridor. Payne trailed along behind, his hands in his pockets, looking this way and that, like a bored schoolboy on a day trip.

'When was your last visit?' Christina asked.

'He fancies you, did you know that?' Payne nodded over his shoulder at Sir Reginald, who was bringing up the rear. 'Old Bald Eagle back there,' Payne continued. 'You can tell just by looking at him.'

'Shut up, Harry,' Christina instructed. 'This is not a game. When were you last here?'

'Three days ago, just like it says in the log.'

'And what was Charlie's state of mind when you left?'

'His usual zombie self. Lost in his own little world.'

'Any progress at all?'

'None that I could tell. Why?'

'Some time last night a security guard with more hormones than sense tried to take Charlie to a little party. Might have gotten away with it too, except he put on the wrong tape. He triggered the killing response. You'll be pleased to know that Charlie responded with absolute effectiveness.'

Payne whistled. 'What was the body count?'

'Three. Through there.' Christina stopped and indicated the double doors leading to the screening room. 'We kept it for you,' she said.

'How considerate. Where's Charlie now?'

Christina shrugged. 'You tell us?' She opened the doors and Payne stepped through.

Once inside the room Payne stood very still. The room was set up just the same as always. The cameras, the video screens, the mattress, all as it should be. Except for the bodies. They were a new addition. And the vibrations. The glorious, primal vibrations. They came at him like a hurricane, battering away at his senses, taking his breath away, too many to cope with. Payne swayed on his feet, dizzy, and reached into his pocket. He came up with a small blue pill which he placed on his tongue, bit forcefully in two and then swallowed. A warm, calm centre began to grow inside him, strengthening, soothing, putting him in control. The vibrations took more coherent shape, delicious now rather than overpowering. He turned very slowly and looked back. He could see Meres looking through the round glass panel in the upper part of the thick double doors. Payne smiled and licked his lips.

Outside in the corridor, Meres turned away in disgust.

'Bloody little bicycle saddle sniffer!' he said, and walked stiffly away.

It was more than an hour later when Payne joined Christina in the Director's office. His face was pale and drawn, but the ghost of a smile haunted his lips.

'Well?' Christina asked. 'How was it for you?'

'Almost as good as being there,' Payne purred.

Christina began to pace back and forth. 'All your reports showed that he was burnt out, incapable of the killing response. How the hell could he suddenly go berserk like this?' she demanded.

'I said he was resisting specific programming,' Payne countered. 'Given the right stimulus, anyone is capable of the killing response. Even you.'

The last two words were soft, weighted. Christina blushed.

'Don't push your luck, Harry,' she whispered. 'Just tell me where you think he's gone.'

Payne laughed. 'Who says he's gone anywhere? He could be right under your nose and you wouldn't suspect a thing. He could even be me. Or you. How could you tell?'

Christina leaned across the table, bringing her face very close to him and speaking with barely suppressed rage.

'This is not a game,' she told him.

'What do you want me to do?' Payne asked, his voice soft, reasonable.

Christina cleared her throat. 'I want you to find him,' she said.

'And after I find him?'

'He's a valuable asset, Harry. Your prime objective is to retrieve him for future use.'

'And if he doesn't want to come back?'

'Then retire him.'

Payne smiled at the euphemism.

However you put it, the Juggler had just passed a death sentence on Charlatan.

Chapter 7

What have I done?

What have I done?

Deep down inside, Charlie knew what he'd done. He didn't know where he was or where he was going, but he knew what he'd done all right.

It was the bad thing.

It hadn't started out that way. At first it had been the sexy thing. Charlie didn't like that either, but it was better than the bad thing. But he was so tired. He just couldn't do it. He 'made the face' like they asked. That's what they used to say to him when he was young.

'Make a face, Charlie, make a face.'

And he would. Any face they wanted, and they'd be so pleased and tell him what a good boy he was. So he made the face for them, but that wasn't enough. The sexy tape was running, but he had no energy, and the lady started to laugh at him and he felt so ashamed.

Then the big man started to hit him and call him names, and Charlie felt the anger build inside him. He wouldn't have given in to it, no matter what they did, if only the other man hadn't changed the tape. It was the Bad Man's special tape. The one he always used when he wanted Charlie to do the bad thing.

'Do you play chess?'

That's how it always started.

When Charlie heard that voice he screamed, tried to tell them, begged them to turn it off.

They hadn't listened.

The big man had just kept on hitting him.

And everything turned red.

He remembered hurting the big man with his bare hands. The lady screamed and pulled something from her pocket. Something sharp.

Charlie slapped his hands over his eyes and tried to rub away the memory of what came next.

'Hey, you.' The voice startled Charlie out of his nightmare reverie. The owner of the voice stood over him, a youth of about nineteen or twenty, with ripped denims and a scuffed leather jacket. Charlie blinked and took in his surroundings as if for the first time.

It was dark and the air was stale and cold. Bright street lights illuminated the dirty pavement. People hurried by, on foot or in cars. Charlie was huddled in a shop doorway.

'You can't stay there,' the voice told him. 'The pigs will pick you up for sure.'

'Pigs?' Charlie shivered. This didn't look like a farmyard.

'You got anywhere to go?' the youth asked.

Charlie shook his head.

'Got any money?'

Charlie patted his pockets absently. His new-found acquaintance laughed.

'Don't bother,' he said, 'I can see you haven't. Come on, let's get out of here.'

He held out his hand and helped Charlie to his feet.

'I'm Stevey,' he said. 'You got a name?'

Charlie thought hard. He'd always been told not to give his real name to strangers. Only give the pretend name. But this time he had no pretend name.

'I . . . I . . .' he stammered.

'Skip it. I'll just call you John, okay?'

Charlie nodded.

'Terrific. Come on, John, let's find something to eat.'

The food was greasy and the tea was strong. Charlie wolfed it down in huge mouthfuls.

'Slow down,' Stevey advised. 'You'll choke yourself. When did you last eat, anyway?'

Charlie shrugged. Yesterday? Last week? He had no idea what day this was. The question was just too difficult, so he ignored it and continued to shovel food into his mouth.

Stevey laughed softly. 'You on the run?' he asked.

Charlie paused, fork half-way between plate and mouth.

'Don't worry,' Stevey assured him. 'We're all on the run from something. Go on, eat.'

Charlie did as he was told. When he had finished Stevey offered him a cigarette. He refused politely.

'No, thank you,' he said. 'They're bad for you.'

'Oh yeah?' Stevey smiled and shook his head. 'Boy, can I pick 'em!' He grinned.

Charlie wasn't sure what he meant, but he seemed to think something was funny so he joined in, smiling and laughing. It felt good to laugh.

'So,' Stevey said, 'you have nowhere to go, right?'

Charlie nodded.

'And no money?'

A shake of the head this time.

'Not even a name?'

Another shake.

Stevey snapped his fingers, as though an idea had just struck him. 'Do you like movies?' he asked.

Charlie nodded enthusiastically. It had been so long since they had let him see a real movie.

'Then I know just the place for you,' Stevey continued. 'Come on.' He took him by the arm and led him into the night.

The Video Dome.

It used to be a meat market.

Not much has changed really. A gleaming metal shell and giant video screens hide the bloodstains on the wall. The smell of sweaty bodies and watered-down booze mask the lingering odour of rancid beef. It is the place to go if you want to score. Anything.

There was a queue outside, but Stevey marched straight up to the bouncer on the door, dragging Charlie with him. Stevey whispered something in the man's ear. He nodded and let them pass. Those still waiting voiced their disapproval briefly, too frightened of being ejected from the queue, or worse, to make too much fuss.

Inside it was like a war zone.

The darkness was interrupted by blinding strobe lights. The noise was so loud that Charlie had to put his hands over his ears to try and block it out. And people. He'd never seen so many people, all of them leaping and jerking and twitching, shrapnel victims of the continuous sound barrage that surrounded them. The air was moist, like breathing through a flannel. Charlie felt the moisture erupt from his pores; his head swam and he felt faint. Stevey nudged him in the ribs and pointed to the video screens high up on the walls.

'Movies, John, dozens of 'em!' he yelled, and laughed.

Charlie looked. They were movies all right. Short clips from them, anyway. Mostly violent shoot 'em ups or kung-fu movies. Some soft porn erotica, depending on what was playing.

Stevey grabbed Charlie by the arm and pulled him through the heaving mass of bodies. He led him to a door beside the bar marked Staff Only and pushed him through. With the door shut behind them, the noise eased off slightly. Stevey grinned, his face damp with sweat.

'Some place, huh, John?' he asked.

He didn't seem to need an answer. Stevey turned and led the way upstairs. The further they climbed the fainter the noise became. For that Charlie was grateful. At the top of the stairs was a long corridor with various doors leading off from it. By the time they reached the door at the very end the noise had been reduced to a dull vibration running through the floor and into the soles of their feet. Stevey paused outside the door.

'You want a place to stay and money in your pocket?' he asked.

Charlie nodded dumbly. It seemed to be the correct response.

'Then just be cool,' Stevey advised. 'Go along with whatever Rick says and everything will be fine, okay?'

Charlie nodded again. His head hurt and he felt drained. All he wanted was his bed back at Denby. If he couldn't have that, and some small part of his mind told him that his actions had made that impossible now, then maybe this would be just as good. Maybe this Rick person was a doctor. The doctors at Denby had told Charlie what to do all the time. He didn't always like it, but if he did what he was told, sometimes they gave him a treat. Perhaps this would be the same.

Stevey knocked on the door. From inside a voice said:

'Come!'

Rick Jarvis stood up as his visitors entered.

He was a slightly built man of forty-eight who tried to disguise his age by combing his thinning hair into a ponytail and dressing 'young'.

'Slick' Rick Jarvis was a man with a mission. He wanted to make people happy. Give the punter what he wants, whatever that may be, had always been his motto. That way he'll always be happy. Along the way that philosophy had made Richard Alexander Jarvis a very rich man, and that was just fine with Slick Rick.

'Steven!' he said, coming from behind his desk and shaking hands warmly. 'How nice to see you again. And you've brought a little friend. How charming. Do introduce us.'

'Rick, this is John. John, meet Rick.'

Charlie took the proffered hand by reflex action.

'John?' Rick mused. 'A good, solid, dependable name. Do you have another one to go with it?'

Charlie blinked. He knew he was being asked a question, but he couldn't figure out what it was. Stevey replied for him.

'Just John,' he said.

'Charming,' Rick continued. 'Do sit down, John, you look all in.'

Charlie sank thankfully into a large, padded armchair. His stomach was jumping now, the fried food he had eaten earlier coming back to plague him. His limbs felt heavy and his head hurt. He could hear voices, the muted buzz of conversation, but the words were indistinct. His head felt like it was coming apart and being put back together again all at the same time.

Rick knelt in front of him, his face close. He smelt of perfume.

'Stevey tells me you have no place to go,' he said. 'Is that right?'

Charlie nodded.

'Would you like to stay here? I have a spare room that "friends" sometimes use. Would you like that, John?'

Charlie nodded again. 'Yes please,' he managed.

'Good.' Rick positively beamed. 'I think we're going to get along splendidly. Stevey tells me you like movies. Is that true?'

Charlie smiled. 'Yes, I like movies very much.'

'How would you like to be in your very own movie, John? Would you enjoy that? I can make that happen, you know. Do you want me to make it happen for you?'

The images were coming too fast for Charlie to cope with. A movie? He nodded, dumbfounded.

Rick smiled again and stood up. 'Excellent,' he said. He turned to Stevey. 'Get him ready and bring him through for his "screen test",' he instructed, and patted Stevey's cheek. 'You really are a wicked boy,' he whispered. 'Don't ever change.'

Rick left the office. His footsteps receded, then a door opened and closed.

Stevey grinned a big Cheshire Cat grin.

'Congratulations,' he said. 'Fame and fortune await. Don't just sit there. Take your clothes off.'

Chapter 8

At least it's not stripping.

So how come I still end up naked in public?

Molly pondered the question that had dogged her since she had sprouted a thirty-six-inch chest at the age of fourteen. At first it had been the boys in the playground. Then the numerous 'Uncles' her mother had brought home. Even her boss at the dead-end factory job she'd taken at sixteen. All of them had wanted to get Molly to shed her clothes. Finally she'd decided that, if this was going to be the pattern of her life, she may as well get paid for it.

She became a stripper at eighteen. Just for a year or two, she told herself, then I'll move on. Modelling maybe, or acting. Ten years later she was still 'getting 'em off' in grimy working men's clubs, dodging the groping, sweaty punters and kidding herself it was only temporary.

And then Mike Menagerie had offered her a chance to get into show-biz for real. At first she thought he was just shooting a line, with his obviously fake name, drooping moustache and 'seventies fashion sense. But he persisted, and Molly began to feel flattered by the attention. He gave her a crumpled flyer advertising Lookalike's next gig and asked her to come along. Why not? she thought. She had nothing to do that night, and anyway it might be fun.

Molly first saw them play in a cramped back-street pub, and they were really quite good. Dressing up as famous people was fun. She'd been doing it herself for some years now, pretending to be Marilyn, giving ageing Teddy Boys the cheap thrill of a lifetime as they watched their boyhood wet dream come alive in front of their eyes. But she was bored with that, and the money was lousy. And she really could sing!

There and then Molly made up her mind that this was going to be her big break. No more stripping. Mike swore, hand on heart, that she would get to keep her clothes on.

He'd lied, of course.

Lookalike played the fourth-division clubs and pubs. The more Molly took off, the easier it was to get a repeat booking. Normally she only had to strip to a sexy basque or stockings and suspenders. If it was an important gig then she'd twirl her tassels, but now and then, like the Hellfire Club, she had to go all the way. The thought of it still made her shudder.

Everyone was mad at Mike, but Molly felt sorry for him. He tried so hard, even if he was a lying little shit.

With the gear smashed they'd had to cancel some gigs, which was bad news. They had just four weeks before they started a summer season at a holiday camp, and no money coming in. That's why Molly was here. Stark naked, but not stripping. Posing for the local art class didn't pay very well, but at least it was something.

She stood on a platform, balancing a vase on one shoulder in a vaguely Grecian pose. Twelve painters daubed away at rickety easels while the teacher, a hatchet-faced woman called Miss Winter, peered through half-moon spectacles and advised on colour tone. A two-bar electric fire tried, and failed, to keep the chill out of the room. Molly felt the goose-bumps break out on her arms.

Miss Winter prodded her in the thigh with one sharp fingernail.

'Keep that knee bent,' she ordered. 'How can anyone paint you if you keep fidgeting so?'

Molly gritted her teeth and did as she was told.

'I will not be doing this for the rest of my life,' she told herself. 'Or stripping. God, even Butlins is better than this!'

The bus stopped opposite the back entrance to Video Dome.

Lookalike had played one of their talent nights here once.

They hadn't won, but Molly had been offered a solo contract to star in a hard-core remake of *The Seven Year Itch*. Her reply to Slick Rick Jarvis had cast doubts upon his parentage for three generations. His theatrical parting shot was that old stand-by, 'You'll never work in this town again!'

Only in his dreams did Rick Jarvis have that sort of clout. Ironic to think that Lookalike now seemed to have made his threat come true.

Molly's bedsit was just three streets away. She paused momentarily, wondering if she had enough money for a drink. Her muscles ached from posing and she was keyed up. A drink might help her sleep.

As she considered her options, a sharp metallic clang drew her attention to the alley that ran down the side of Video Dome. Glancing up, she saw the fire door on the top floor crash open. A figure rushed out and hurtled down the metal ladder, footsteps ringing in the cold night air. Whoever it was, was in a hurry. Too much of a hurry. Molly gasped as he stumbled and fell the last six feet, landing face down on the alley floor. He lay still, winded, or worse.

Molly quickly crossed the street. The figure twitched and tried to sit up just as heavy, crashing footsteps sounded from above.

'Get away from him!' someone yelled. 'That bastard is mine!'

Molly recognised the voice, although now it was choked with rage. She looked up and gasped. Rick Jarvis didn't look so slick any more. His ponytail was loose, wispy hair flying around his face as he ran. His shirt was ripped and splattered with the blood that ran freely from his nose. In his hand he carried a knife.

The figure on the ground struggled to a sitting position. In the dim light Molly couldn't see him clearly, but he looked young and very frightened. A nice face, she decided. Without the fear and the pain it would be a very nice face, with large soulful eyes and delicate features.

He looked so helpless lying there that Molly wanted to gather him up and make it all better. Rick Jarvis, on the other hand, wanted to carve his initials in the face that Molly found so appealing.

Jarvis jumped the last three steps, landed heavily and shoved Molly aside.

'Fuck off!' he screamed at her. 'This is private. Understand?'

He looked at her for the first time and his eyes narrowed.

'I know you,' he said.

Molly nodded, her heart racing like a hamster on a treadmill.

'I . . . uh . . . we played here once,' she stammered.

Please God, don't let him remember what I called him.

Jarvis wiped blood from his lips with the back of his hand.

'Yeah,' he drawled, 'I remember. You were crap. And when I tried to do you a favour you called me a bastard son of a junkie whore!'

Thanks a bunch, God!

'Ungrateful bitch!' he yelled. 'Just like this bastard.' He lashed out with his foot, catching Charlie in the stomach, flipping him over onto his back with a grunt of pain.

'Hey!' Molly yelled and rushed forward.

Jarvis swivelled to meet her, the knife inches from her face. She stopped dead in her tracks.

'You see this?' he screamed, pointing to his face with his free hand. 'You see what this bastard did to me? And Stevey.' He paused, and Molly could swear there were tears in his eyes. 'He broke his arms,' Jarvis continued. 'Both of them! That ungrateful son of a bitch broke both his arms and did this to my face. Now it's his turn.'

With a snarl Jarvis turned back to the prone figure and leaned forward.

Molly's next action was instinctive. She didn't stop to think, just raced forward, reached both hands between Jarvis's legs, grabbed hold of his genitals and squeezed as hard as she could.

Jarvis's whole body quivered. He screamed falsetto, like a castrated pig. Encouraged by his reaction, Molly heaved upward with all her might. For a split second, Jarvis danced on tiptoe in a vain effort to relieve the pressure, then he gave in to his fate and performed a complete somersault, landing heavily on his back. The knife clattered from his hand. He rolled himself into a foetal position, groaning loudly, his hands clamped between his thighs.

Molly moved quickly to Jarvis's intended victim. She grabbed him by the arm and hauled him to his feet.

'Can you walk?' she asked urgently.

He nodded.

'Great,' she said. 'How about running? I think we just outstayed our welcome!'

Chapter 9

Rufus was black, but that was the least of his problems.

He was old, too, but that was a cross everyone had to bear if they lived long enough.

The fact that he smelt and was filthy he regarded as a personal hygiene statement that people could accept or not. The choice was theirs.

The rheumatism was a curse, but with enough rum inside him he could almost forget that. Oh yes, Rufus was also an alcoholic. He didn't regard that as a problem, more a fact of life.

The night was just getting cold enough to make him look forward to his bed at the hostel. He had his route all planned. Down Neptune Road, then left onto Queen Elizabeth Street which led down to the docks. Rufus liked to see what ships were in port. They reminded him of his trip over from Jamaica in 1947. Lots of things had changed since then, of course, and not all of them for the better, but Rufus wasn't one of those given to crying over spilt milk. He liked to look at the ships, and that was that. Then he'd make his way across the park to the St James Hostel. Should take about an hour at his regular shambling pace.

He was half-way down Canute Road when he saw a sight that changed his plans. He saw a woman, half-carrying, half-dragging a man who looked like he had passed out. She was struggling under the weight, breathing heavily and cursing under her breath. As she drew nearer Rufus recognised her and called out.

'Hey, Molly,' he called, 'you got to mug 'em now before they'll come home with you?' Rufus cackled at his own wit.

Molly paused, propped her unwieldy burden against a lamp-post and waved Rufus closer.

'Stop taking the piss, you old toss-pot,' she gasped, 'and give me a hand.'

Rufus sauntered casually closer, taking his own sweet time.

'Since you ask so nice,' he said, 'I'll see what I can do. Where you goin' anyways?'

'To a bleedin' garden party! Where do you think I'm going this time of night? Home, of course.'

Rufus considered the situation. Molly lived in a bedsit half-way down Canute Road.

'You want me to help you get him back to your place?' Rufus asked.

'If it's not too much trouble, Rufus, yes!'

'That's a long way, girl.'

37

'It's barely fifty feet, Rufus!'

'But it's two floors up. That's an awful lot of stairs for a man in my condition.'

'I'll make a deal with you, Rufus. Help me get him inside and I'll massage away all your aches and pains. Or I'll give you the price of a nightcap. Which do you want?'

'Can't I have both?'

Molly shook her head. 'Life's a bitch, Rufus,' she told him. 'You have to choose.'

Rufus licked his lips and laughed. 'If I was twenty years younger, girl,' he said.

'But you're not,' Molly told him. 'So take his arm, for God's sake, before we all end up in the gutter.'

Rufus laboriously did as he was told, taking some of the weight from Molly's shoulders. He wrinkled his nose in distaste.

'Phew!' he said, 'he stinks.'

'That's rich, coming from you!' Molly muttered.

Rufus eyed some fresh stains with an expert eye. 'He been sick?' he asked.

'Yes,' Molly hissed, 'he's been sick. Twice, if you must know.'

'Jesus God, girl, what you been doin' to him?'

'I haven't been doing anything to him! If you must know, I saved him from having his face ripped off by some nutter with a carving knife. We were running like buggery when he suddenly stopped, threw up, twice, and practically collapsed. I don't even know his name.'

'And now you're taking him home?'

'Yes, Rufus, now I'm taking him home. Any objections?'

'Didn't know you were so desperate for some company, Molly.'

'Just shut up, Rufus. Just shut up, okay?'

Rufus shut up. Except for a string of moans and groans as they manhandled their burden up to Molly's front door. Molly fumbled the key into the lock and they practically fell over the threshold. With a lot of grunting and swearing they tipped their cargo onto Molly's bed. Rufus leaned against the wall and mopped his brow.

'Need a hand to get him undressed, Molly?' he asked, his eyes twinkling with mischief.

'If I decide I want him undressed, Rufus, I think I can manage that on my own, don't you?'

Rufus grinned. 'If you say so, Molly, if you say so.'

'I do say so. Thanks for your help, Rufus. Here, take this.' Molly rummaged in her purse for some loose change.

'I don't want your money, Molly!' Rufus protested. 'We're friends, you and me.'

'A deal's a deal, Rufus. Take it.' She pressed some coins into his hand.

'You're a good person, Molly, a real good person.'
'I'll remember that if I ever need a reference.'
Rufus shuffled towards the door, and then stopped.
'Molly,' he said, 'you're not in any trouble, are you?'
Molly sighed. 'Probably,' she admitted. 'But nothing I can't handle.'
'Anythin' I can do?'
'You've done enough, Rufus. Really. Thanks a lot.'
'Just you take care now, girl, you hear me?'
'I hear you, Rufus, I hear you.'
Molly ushered him out, waved him goodbye and closed and locked the door. She leant against it, catching her breath, watching the still figure lying on her bed.
'What the hell have I got myself into?' she asked herself.
The only reply was a gentle snore.
Molly removed his shoes and his shirt. The latter she put into soak to try and get the worst of the stains out. She covered him with a blanket. He was curled up on his side, sucking his thumb. Molly brushed a strand of loose hair from his eyes.
'Just like a big baby,' she murmured.
Christ, don't get broody all of a sudden, she told herself.
Looking down at him she found it difficult to believe he could have maimed two people earlier that evening. But then she only had Rick Jarvis's word for that. Looking at him now he looked like he couldn't hurt a fly.
Once she was sure he was comfortable, Molly went into the bathroom, slipped off her clothes, showered and wrapped herself in a large bathrobe. Then she pulled her only armchair close to the bed, curled up in it and nodded off to sleep.

Chapter 10

In the schoolboy vernacular of the Secret Service, Joseph Chamberlain was known as Warlord. It was a particularly robust appellation that gave him absurd pleasure. His more prosaic official title, Controller of Specialised Services, better known as S1, carried none of the *joie de vivre* of his preferred nickname. Neither one portrayed the true nature of his work, of course. In truth he was a procurer, a provider of the people and services needed to protect the nation's interest, whatever they might be.

Warlord had been pimping for Her Majesty's Government for more than forty years. Well past the mandatory age of retirement for those in his line of work, he had been allowed to stay on because his expertise was considered to be of 'unique and invaluable importance in these stringent times'. That was how they had phrased it in the official letter that extended his tenure. In short, Warlord knew where too many bodies were buried for anyone to want to take the risk of removing him from office before he was prepared to go. Even so, with his sixty-fifth birthday a matter of months away, he knew his stay of execution was almost up. After so many years in harness the idea had even started to have some appeal. And then this Charlatan business had blown up. It would not make a fitting end to an illustrious career.

Charlatan's file lay open on his desk. He didn't look at it. He knew it word for word. It had been Chamberlain who had discovered Charlatan when he was still a child; discovered him, trained him and controlled his operations personally for many years. The so-called experts had never truly been able to define exactly what Charlatan's powers were. One particularly earnest young doctor had opined that Charlatan was '... a genetic anomaly with an unstable DNA structure that reacted to adrenal surges as a defence mechanism in much the same way as a chameleon will change the colour of its skin in order to blend in with its background ...'

It was gobbledegook, of course. In plain English, Charlatan was a shape changer. The man could actually manipulate the muscles and bones of his body at will; make them assume any shape he chose, change the colour of his skin pigmentation, even the length and colour of his hair. He could even change sex. It always gave Warlord an unholy thrill to watch Charlatan change from a man to a woman. This lack of permanent gender identity had led his doctors to the conclusion that Charlatan was sterile. Not that that stopped them from trying to breed from him. In fact, they'd been in the process of exhaustive experiments to achieve that end when Charlatan had decided to go AWOL. Laboratory tests and artificial insemination had all proved futile, and so they had moved on to live subjects. Prurient interest vied with scientific detachment as a string of willing young women were provided for Charlatan to copulate with, all under the watchful eye of the video camera and a cheering gallery of dedicated scientists.

Warlord was dismissive of their methods and motives. He didn't care whether Charlatan was sterile or not. All he cared about was getting him back into the field as quickly as possible. Now, of course, that might not be possible. Charlatan had always been the most malleable of operatives, his curious elasticity of body mirrored by a mind that could be programmed much as you would programme a computer. His recent reluctance to co-operate had been unusual and annoying; now it was a potential nightmare.

Warlord slammed the file shut, closing the door on his reverie, and focused his attention on Christina Laker. She sat, patiently but tense, returning his gaze levelly, anxious to be gone, to be out there doing her job. It had been three days since the 'Pierce Incident', as it was referred to, and each successive day that passed made Christina's task that much harder. She was an extremely effective Juggler, that's why Warlord had chosen her above many more obvious contenders. He made a point of always choosing his key operatives personally. Christina, Payne, Charlatan, they were all his protégés. It hurt now to have to set them upon each other, but the options were limited.

'Sammy Pierce was a low-life little shite,' Warlord declared. Christina remained silent, neither agreeing nor disagreeing. 'I take it,' Warlord continued, 'that measures have been taken to ensure he troubles us no more in death as he did in life?'

Christina nodded. 'The official story is a fire, due to faulty equipment. Pierce and Sadler perished in the course of their duty and appropriate compensation will be paid to any dependants.'

'And their playmate?'

'She was a working girl. They move on all the time. She won't be missed.'

Warlord considered for a moment. 'Good,' he said. 'What are the chances of Charlatan going public?'

'That's unlikely, sir.'

'But not impossible?'

'Nothing is impossible, sir, but it's highly improbable.'

'Not a premeditated escape on his part then?'

'Absolutely not. He simply blew a fuse. I doubt if he even realised what he was doing. He was subjected to an unauthorised and unsupervised simulation exercise and reacted accordingly.'

'He could still prove embarrassing if his knowledge fell into the wrong hands.'

'Over the last year Charlatan has regressed to a childlike state. Any information he still retains is fragmented, insupportable. It would be regarded as the ramblings of a madman.'

'Are you certain of that?'

'Positive.'

Warlord paused. 'Let's hope you're right,' he said at last, 'for all our sakes. You do know, I suppose, that Meres has put in a formal complaint against the way you handled this operation.'

'I guessed as much.'

'Says you ignored his advice and had a blatant disregard for procedures.'

'If he means that I was achieving results where he had consistently failed, then he's right. Sir.' The last word was an afterthought.

Warlord gave a snort of laughter. He liked women with spirit, and Christina was a prime example. However, things had been screwed up on a large scale and someone had to carry the can. At the moment that looked like being Christina Laker.

'Can the situation be rectified?' he asked.

'I believe so, sir. With time.'

'You don't have any time, Christina. This has to be settled quickly and quietly. You understand the reasons why as well as I do, don't you?'

Christina nodded. The use of such volatile individuals as Payne and Charlatan in live situations was officially forbidden. The fact that Warlord had been doing just that for almost a quarter of a century had been conveniently overlooked as long as he achieved the desired results. If the current situation went public some serious questions would be asked. Questions that could not be answered.

'Then we understand each other, Christina,' he continued. 'Payne is a good man, but he needs watching. I know that better than anyone. Keep him at it, Christina. I want this mess sorted out inside a week.'

Chapter 11

Humpty Dumpty sat on a wall
Humpty Dumpty had a great fall
All the King's horses
And all the King's men
Couldn't put Humpty together again.

What's happened to my house?
Someone's been here, knocking down the walls.
The Bad Man?
Who's he?
Never mind, you don't want to know.
Someone else then, because the walls are all knocked down.
I'm just like Humpty now, all in pieces that don't seem to fit.
Where am I?
Who am I?

'Good morning. Would you like some breakfast?'

Charlie's stomach growled. The lady smiled.

'I'll take that as a yes,' she said. 'My name's Molly.' She stuck out her hand. Charlie flinched. A look of concern crossed her face.

'Hey, don't worry,' she said. 'I'm not going to hurt you. I'm one of the good guys. I'm the cavalry who came over the hill last night, remember?'

Charlie smiled. 'Like John Wayne?' he asked.

Where did that thought come from?

Molly laughed. It was a nice sound.

'I suppose I've been called worse things,' she said. 'You still haven't told me your name.'

Charlie thought hard. His mind was in so many pieces.

Humpty Dumpty.

'Charlatan,' he said. That piece seemed to fit.

Molly looked quizzical. 'Is that a name?' she asked.

He nodded. 'It's my name. Friends call me Charlie.'

'Charlie it is, then. What would you like for breakfast, Charlie?'

Humpty Dumpty time again.

Which piece has breakfast on it?

'Don't worry,' she told him. 'I'll improvise. Okay?' She smiled.

He nodded and returned the smile with a shy grin. Molly disappeared into the kitchen. Charlie watched her go. She was nice, he decided.

43

He could hear her moving about in the kitchen, rattling cups and saucers, humming to herself.

Can I stay here? he wondered. Wherever 'here' is. He sat up in bed, hugging his knees to his chest. He felt very small and empty, his thoughts a kaleidoscope of fractured images, some good, some bad and some terrible. The terrible ones he pushed away, trying to lose them in the multicoloured jumble that passed for his mind. Some things he knew by instinct, though he didn't know how he came to know them. He knew the thing he was sitting on was called a bed, and just knowing this simple fact delighted him somehow. He pushed the mattress with his hand.

'Bed,' he said, as though practising a foreign language.

'Did you say something?' Molly called from the kitchen.

'Uh . . . nice bed,' he replied.

She laughed. 'Thanks. Do you like music?'

Do I? Humpty Dumpty.

'Yes?' Charlie wasn't certain, but he thought he probably did.

'Okay,' Molly replied. Charlie heard a click and music filtered through from the other room. He didn't precisely know how it could do that, but it didn't worry him. 'I'll remember,' he told himself. Just got to find the right pieces.

Molly was busying herself getting cereals, toast, marmalade and tea. It was nice to have someone to fuss over, even a complete stranger. In a way, that made it more exciting. Despite how they'd met. Despite what Jarvis had said, she didn't feel threatened by him. Just the opposite, and Molly prided herself on being a good judge of character. He needs someone to look after him, that's all, she told herself.

On the radio the distinctive opening chords of 'Jailhouse Rock' replaced the morning DJ's puerile cheerfulness. Molly began to hum along. From next door she heard Charlie start to join in with the chorus. At least he sounded cheerful. Molly stopped midway through buttering a slice of toast and listened carefully. He had a good voice, but there was something more. Molly moved to the doorway, butter knife in hand. Charlie was sitting, hunched up in her bed, staring at a Mickey Mouse poster on the opposite wall. She kept it there so she would have something cheerful to look at as soon as she opened her eyes each morning. Charlie was staring at it, smiling and singing along. Molly frowned. What was it about his voice? She reached out and turned the sound down on the radio. Charlie stopped abruptly and turned to look at her. She smiled encouragingly. 'Don't stop,' she said. 'You have a nice voice; I'd just like to listen to you by yourself for a while.'

Charlie beamed. 'Really?' he said.

'Sure. Don't be shy, carry on singing.'

Charlie picked up the tune from where he had left off. To his surprise he found he could remember the words quite easily. As Molly listened, her eyes grew wide and her mouth gaped.

He sounded identical!

I mean, most people think they can sing like Elvis, some are even pretty good, but most do a version of what Presley was like. But not Charlie. Charlie was note perfect, pitch, tone, inflection, just like listening to the record without the music!

Molly laughed and bounced onto the bed. Charlie stopped singing, uncertain as to what this reaction meant.

'You're brilliant!' she told him.

'I am?'

'Where did you learn to do that?'

Charlie shrugged. 'I don't know, it just came to me.'

'You could make a fortune with a voice like that!' She stopped herself. '*We* could make a fortune!' she corrected.

'How?' This conversation was starting to slip from Charlie's grasp. Whatever happened to breakfast?

'I know someone who's going to be very pleased to see you,' she told him. 'I'm meeting him this evening. In the meantime, let's have breakfast. Then you can tell me your entire life history!'

Chapter 12

The room was quite small. A desk, two chairs, a TV and video were its
only furnishings. The desk top was bare, save for an ashtray and a chessboard set up with a game in progress. In the corner a large stack of
papers and video tapes lay in an untidy heap. Newspapers, maga-
zines, periodicals and copies of police reports, all from a hundred
miles' radius of the Hampshire village of Denby.

Payne sat behind the desk. He was concentrating on the chessboard over steepled fingers. 'Come in, Christina,' he called. The
door opened, as if on cue, and Christina entered. 'Very clever,' she
muttered. Payne grinned and raised his eyes from the chessboard,
letting his gaze travel slowly up her body. He had cruel, feverish eyes,
and whenever he looked at her like that, Christina felt stripped, not
just naked, but right down to the bone. She blushed for no good reason and cursed him under her breath. He was the only man who could
make her blush and she didn't like it one bit.

'I need a progress report,' she said. 'Our Masters are getting the jit-
ters.'

'Your Masters, not mine. Would you care for a game? I do so enjoy
chess, don't you?'

Christina pulled up a chair and sat down. Her gaze fell upon the ashtray. It was full of small blue pills.

'I see you've stopped taking the tablets.' she observed, and moved a
pawn. Payne promptly took it with his knight.

'I need to be sharp,' he told her. 'Very sharp. The pills give me a
measure of control, but they also dull the edge.'

'Just don't get too sharp, Harry, you may cut yourself.'

'And if I do, we both bleed, correct?'

'Something like that. What can I tell them, Harry? That you're watching TV and reading the papers?' She moved her rook to an attacking
position.

'Tell them I'm doing research. He could be anywhere, but when he
surfaces, chances are he'll make the news. He's that sort of person.'

'He had no money, no ID, no nothing. How far could he have got?'

Payne shrugged. 'He was trained by the best,' he said. 'Me!' He
grinned. 'Combined with his natural talent, if he remembers half of
what he knows, the world is his oyster.'

'Isn't there some way you can "tune in" on him, track him down?'

'My dear Tina, I'm not a bloodhound! Believe me, this is the best
way.'

Payne moved his bishop horizontally across the board.

'That's an illegal move, Harry,' Christina observed. 'You can't do that.'

Payne sighed and leant forward, palms flat on either side of the board.

'I thought you understood?' he said. 'Chess is so much like life. A game of subterfuge and deceit. We sacrifice pawns when we must to protect our king at all costs. And those who play by the rules inevitably lose.'

Christina stood up. 'We're all pawns, Harry. Even you.'

'Is that a threat, Tina? If so, it's unworthy of you.'

'Just a word to the wise, Harry. Warlord wants results. If he doesn't get them we'll both be removed from the arena of operations. I've stuck my neck out for you in the past, Harry. Don't let me down now.' Christina moved her queen. 'Checkmate,' she said.

Chapter 13

It was still early. The Cellar was only half full. For a basement pub it was aptly named. It was a favourite haunt for aspiring musicians, with live music three nights a week, and the wall hung with pictures of the famous and near-famous.

Mike Menagerie sat in a corner booth nursing a pint of Guinness. Billy sat opposite him.

'I don't want to be a bloody butcher!' Mike said for the umpteenth time.

'So don't be one,' Billy replied wearily. 'Tell your old lady to bugger off. If she doesn't like it, move out.'

'Serve her right if I did. But she needs me, you see. She's not well. I can't just abandon her, she's me Mum.'

Billy nodded without much sympathy. The only thing wrong with Doreen Smith was a bad case of overprotectiveness. She was a large, robust woman, strong as an ox, but skilled at using her hypochondria to ensure her loving son didn't run out on her the way his father had done. Mike, it seemed, took after his father in both looks and personality. Philip Smith had been a petty thief until he married Doreen. She soon put him on the straight and narrow, ruling the roost with a fist of iron. Phil had put up with it long enough to see his son born, and then scarpered while mother and child were still in hospital and incapable of doing anything about it. Mike had been paying for his father's indiscretion ever since. Everyone could see it, except Mike himself. Most people considered it pathetic, especially for someone with such grand ideas about being a showbiz legend.

'Where the hell is she?' Mike asked, changing the subject. 'I said half seven, and look at it now, nearly eight. Where is she?'

Billy shrugged. 'No idea,' he said. 'Doesn't matter much though, does it? We've not exactly got good news for her, have we?'

Mike gave him a sour look and took a pull on his pint.

Billy took a deep breath. Over the last few weeks there had been a long-running argument between them.

'Why don't we try something different?' Billy argued. 'If you'd just listen to some of the numbers I've written . . .'

'We've got a reputation to think of,' Mike countered. 'We're a name band.' It was only a white lie. 'We can't bugger things up just because you think you're the next Paul McCartney!'

'I never said I was! If you'd just listen.'

'I need a piss,' Mike announced, and left the table, effectively end-ing the conversation.

'Bastard!' Billy muttered. 'Stupid, stubborn, mummy's boy bastard!'

Mike Menagerie stood at the urinal, relieving himself and staring up at the ceiling. If only all of life's problems could be solved as easily as having a piss, things would be a hell of a lot simpler.

He knew he was just being stubborn. Billy was a good musician, but trying to break a new band was not easy. Lookalike traded on the nostalgia boom, and that would never die. It meant money in the bank long-term once they really got known. Besides, Lookalike had been Mike's brainchild and he was reluctant to give up on it.

He zipped himself up and turned to wash his hands, just like his mother had always told him he should, and someone hit him very hard in the stomach.

Lost in his own thoughts, he hadn't even noticed anyone follow him into the toilets, but he was noticing them now. He choked back bile as his knees buckled and he fell to the floor. Someone straddled him and grabbed a handful of his hair, yanking his head back so hard he thought he was being scalped. Blinking tears from his eyes, a face he recognised swam into view.

'Rick!' he gasped. 'What happened to your face?'

Rick Jarvis had two enormous black eyes and a wad of sticking plaster across his face. Over Jarvis's right shoulder Mike saw another face he recognised. Stevey Something, his name was. Both his arms were in slings. Mike couldn't see who was holding his hair, but he guessed it was one of Jarvis's neanderthals, all steroids and bad attitude.

Jarvis ignored Mike's question and leaned closer.

'Where is she?' he asked.

'Who do you mean, Rick?' Mike quavered.

The neanderthal yanked his hair hard enough to lift him off the floor. Mike screamed and tried to prise the fingers loose, but had no effect.

'That bitch of yours,' Jarvis snarled, 'that's who.'

'Molly?' Mike gasped.

'That's the one. I want her and you're going to tell me where to find her.'

'But . . . why?'

Mike knew it was a dumb question as soon as he asked it, but it was too late to retract; the words were already out.

'Why?' Jarvis thundered. 'Why? Because of this!' He pointed towards his own face. 'And because of that.' He pointed towards Stevey's dual slings. 'That's why. That bitch and her boyfriend did this and they're going to pay, do you understand?'

Mike would have nodded if he'd been able. Suddenly his throat was too dry to speak. He didn't even know Molly had a boyfriend!

The door opened and an unwitting customer came in, unzipping his fly as he walked.

'Piss off!' Jarvis shouted. 'It's engaged, all right?'

The customer turned smartly on his heel and disappeared without a word.

'Now,' Jarvis continued. 'Where is she?'

Mike licked his lips, finally dredging up enough spit to speak.

'I don't know,' he squeaked. The grip on his scalp tightened and he moaned. 'Honest, I don't know!' He was frantic now. 'She was meant to be here tonight, but she hasn't shown. I don't know where she is, Rick, honest.'

'You're a lying bastard, Menagerie,' Jarvis informed him. 'Bring him over here.' Jarvis moved to one of the stalls, walking with a peculiar, stiff-legged gait. Mike wondered dully if he'd hurt his foot as well as his face. The neanderthal holding Mike's hair released his grip, only to replace it with one on his neck that threatened to crush his windpipe. Mike found his right arm pulled up sharply between his shoulder blades as he was hauled to his feet and frogmarched into a toilet stall.

A sharp kick to his ankles sent Mike crashing painfully to his knees, his head inches above the lavatory bowl.

Jarvis was standing next to the bowl, his hand on the chain.

'I'll ask you one more time,' he said. 'Where can I find her?'

'Just let me get this straight.'

Charlie groaned. Molly had been quizzing him for what seemed like hours. They were sitting, facing each other cross-legged on Molly's bed. She began ticking off each point on her fingers as she spoke.

'You have no name except Charlatan, right?'

Charlie nodded wearily.

'You have no idea who your parents are, or where you come from?'

'No.'

'You can't remember anything before a couple of days ago when you found yourself sleeping in doorways and eating out of dustbins, right?'

'Right.'

'Jesus! It's like you just fell out of the sky or something.'

'Maybe I did.'

'You don't remember having an accident or anything like that? No knock on the head that could have caused amnesia?'

'I don't remember anything. Except the nightmare.'

'Oh, yeah, this bogie man . . .'

'Bad Man.'

'That's him. And some kind of hospital or something, that you had to get away from.'

'Yes.'

'See, maybe you did have an accident after all. Wouldn't it be great if you found out you were really a millionaire or something?'

'If I was, I think someone would have tried to find me by now, don't you?'

'You're probably right. And you're sure you never met Rick Jarvis before last night?'

Charlie shuddered. 'That much I'm sure of,' he said. 'I'm sorry I hurt him, but he's not a nice person.'

'You can say that again!'

'Will you get into trouble for helping me?'

Molly shrugged. 'Nothing I can't handle.' She hoped she sounded more confident than she felt. The conversation lapsed for a while. Molly found herself staring into his eyes. Such sad eyes. The room was almost dark now; they hadn't bothered to turn on the lights. Charlie's pale skin seemed almost luminous in the shadows. He was really an amazing person. His talent for voices was phenomenal. That's how they had spent most of the day, playing games, testing, seeing how far his talent stretched. As far as Molly could make out, there was no limit! They'd worked their way through her record collection and Charlie was able to mimic every single voice, both male and female! So they switched to the TV, and Charlie had copied all the cartoon voices on the afternoon children's programmes. The clincher for Molly was when he had a conversation with her in a voice that sounded so much like her own she could have sworn she was listening to a tape! Molly had a fit of the giggles at that, which quickly turned to hysterics. The laughter was contagious and they had both ended up rolling on the floor like a couple of kids, until their sides ached.

Molly had never met anyone quite like Charlie before. She felt as if she knew him so well, as though they were old friends, but she really knew absolutely nothing about him. What's more, Charlie seemed unable to fill in the gaps.

Unable or unwilling?

Molly dismissed that thought at once. He has nothing to gain by deceiving me, she told herself. Except a roof over his head. Free food. A bed to sleep in. Someone to share it with. No, that was unworthy. Molly couldn't explain how or why, but she trusted Charlie implicitly, believed every word he said. Someone must know you, she thought to herself. And one day they'll come to claim you. But until then you're mine, and I'm going to keep you safe.

'What are you thinking about?' he asked.

Molly shook her head. 'Nothing important,' she answered.

'Tell me about your life,' he said quietly.

'What?' The request took her by surprise.

'I've told you all I know about me. I'd just like to know something about you, that's all.'

There was a note of sadness in his voice that made Molly want to cry. 'Well, okay,' she said. 'But it's really not a very good story, I warn you.'

'At least you can remember it,' said Charlie simply.

Molly took a deep breath and held it. She really didn't want to do this. She wasn't ashamed of her life, not really. She'd never sold herself for sex, or done drugs, or hurt anybody. Except Rick Jarvis, and you couldn't count that. It was just that, as she ran the film of her life on the screen in her mind, it all seemed somehow sordid and tainted. She was suddenly very conscious of what Charlie would think of her if she told him the truth. I don't want to lose him, she told herself, which was crazy, because she hardly knew him! All Molly knew was that she had to tell him the truth, and then pray it didn't put him off.

'My name is Molly,' she said, letting out her breath in a rush. 'Molly Travis. I'm twenty-seven years old, single and I live alone. Well, I guess you already know that, don't you?'

Charlie nodded. 'Go on, please,' he said.

'My parents split up when I was ten. They used to row a lot. My Dad would get drunk and get violent. One day Mum met me from school and just took me to a different house. I never saw my Dad again. I had lots of 'Uncles' though, if you get my drift?'

Charlie nodded, but it was impossible to tell from his expression whether he really understood or not.

'Anyway,' she continued, 'I hated them all. I was useless at school and miserable at home. So I left both when I was sixteen. Got myself a job and a fleapit all of my own. Things didn't go so good.' She paused, reluctant to move on to the next part. 'So I started working as a stripper.' There, it was out now, her guilty secret. The expression on Charlie's face didn't change. 'You do know what a stripper is, don't you, Charlie? Someone who takes their clothes off in public for money.'

Charlie nodded, his face inscrutable.

'So, anyway, I did that for a long time, but not any more. Now, I'm a singer. Not that the band's doing too well at the moment, but you're going to change all that for us, I can feel it. You're my lucky charm, Charlie.' She grinned at him and he smiled back. Molly shrugged. 'That's it. That's my life. Not very impressive, is it?'

Charlie reached out and touched her hand very gently. 'It's a nice life,' he said.

'You think so?'

'Nice people have nice lives,' he said. It was a simple statement of fact and it made Molly want to cry.

'Come on,' she said, wiping the sniffles away with the back of her hand. 'We're late already.'

Business at The Cellar was picking up when they arrived. It took Molly a few seconds to find Mike and Billy in their corner booth. Pulling Charlie with her, she made her way over to them, grabbed a couple of spare stools, gave one to Charlie and sat down.

'Hi,' she beamed. 'This is Charlie. Charlie, this is Mike and Billy.'

They all nodded a greeting.

'Mike,' Molly said, 'why is your hair wet?'

Mike scowled. 'What the fuck have you been doing to Rick Jarvis?' he asked.

Molly blushed. She felt Charlie tense up and she grabbed his hand reassuringly.

'How did you know about that?' she asked.

'He's looking for you, that's how I know. Jesus, Molly, the guy's a headcase, you know that. You were lucky to get away with it the last time; why go back and break his face? Have you got a death wish or something?'

'I'll handle it, all right?' She had no idea how, but she'd find a way.

'You'd better. And fast, okay?'

Molly nodded and they lapsed into an uneasy silence. No one offered to buy Molly and Charlie a drink.

'So,' Molly said, after a pause, 'what's happening?'

Mike grunted. 'Nothing much,' he said. 'Frank and Davy have quit, that's all.'

'How come?' Molly asked.

'They got better offers,' Mike snarled bitterly. 'Regular wages and better working conditions.'

'Doing what?'

Mike looked sheepish. 'Davy's got a job on the dustcarts and Frank's working for his brother's taxi firm,' he said. 'Some people just aren't cut out for the bright lights,' he concluded.

'But there's no need to panic,' Billy chipped in. 'I can make the keyboards provide the drum and guitar parts. You can fill in on bass, Molly, and all we need is to find another guitarist sometime. We'll get by, though, don't you think?'

Molly nodded. 'Sounds good,' she said, 'and I have the perfect front-man for us.'

'Oh yeah?' Mike sneered. 'Who?'

Molly gestured towards Charlie. 'Ta-daa!' she said, and grinned like a lunatic.

Charlie smiled sheepishly.

Mike and Billy looked at him in stony silence.

'You,' said Mike eventually, 'must be out of your tiny mind.'

Molly was unperturbed. 'Just wait till you hear him sing,' she said. 'Charlie sings more like Elvis than Elvis!'

'That's what they all say,' Mike jeered. 'Prove it.'

'Okay, we will.'

Molly stood up, grabbed Charlie by the hand and marched him resolutely over to the jukebox.

Mike Menagerie was a happy man. Happier than he'd been since he was fourteen years old and Monica Darlington had let him put his hand down her gym shorts. Of course, tonight, the amount of alcohol he had consumed had helped to elevate his spirits somewhat. And it was all because of Charlie. Good old Charlie! Bloody fantastic Charlie, more like it! He sounded so much like the King it was uncanny. 'Course, he also sounded like every other bugger as well! By the end of the evening the pub had given him a standing ovation! Mike thought he had died and gone to rock-'n'-roll heaven. By the time they staggered into the street it was well past closing time. Molly was flushed with excitement and booze; it was Charlie's turn to hold her up now.

'So,' Molly slurred, 'do we have a new lead singer, or don't we?'

'I should sodding well say so,' Mike slurred back. 'You,' he continued, poking Charlie in the chest, 'are a bloody miracle, mate. That's what you are, a bloody miracle.'

Charlie blushed. 'Thank you,' he said.

'Rehearsals as usual tomorrow, then?' Molly asked.

'S'right,' Mike replied. 'And don't be late! We've got a lot of work to do.'

'We'll be there,' said Molly happily. 'Come on, Charlie, let's go home.'

Mike Menagerie scratched his head. Something was bothering him. Something he couldn't quite remember. It had been very important to him earlier in the evening, but what the hell was it?

Suddenly it came back to him.

'Hey, Molly,' he shouted.

Molly turned back, swaying precariously on Charlie's arm.

'Yeah?' she said.

'Don't bother going home,' Mike told her. 'I gave Rick Jarvis your address!'

Chapter 14

Colin was on a mission from God.

He knew it was true because God had told him so.

It had happened when he was trying to tune his battered transistor radio into Virgin 1215. The batteries were going and reception was lousy, but suddenly a voice came through, loud and clear.

'Hey, Colin,' it said. It sounded just like Alan Freeman, but Colin knew it couldn't be, because Alan Freeman didn't work for Virgin 1215.

'Come a bit closer, Colin,' the voice said. 'I've got something to tell you.'

Colin put his ear to the radio and the voice spoke to him for ten minutes. When the one-way conversation ended, Colin had a fierce, bright light in his eyes and a whole new purpose in life.

Cathy Death.

That's a good name.

Or maybe Cathy Vile?

How about Kinky Cath?

Cathy giggled. She'd need a new name when she joined their coven. Was it called a coven? No, a chapter, that was it. Witches have covens, Hell's Angels have chapters.

Cathy couldn't understand why they called it a chapter, since none of them seemed able to read, but she guessed it was probably historical or symbolic or something.

Cathy was fifteen, slim and pretty, and as far as her parents were concerned she was at the Youth Club.

For weeks now Cathy had forgone the pleasures of the Youth Club in favour of an entirely different type of club altogether! She left home as usual, dressed in track-suit and trainers. No one ever questioned what she had in the plastic bag she carried. Had they done so she would have told them it was a sweater, in case it got chilly later on, or maybe some books or records that she was lending to a friend. They would have believed her; they trusted her. Cathy had always been a good little girl.

Cathy prayed for fine weather on Youth Club nights. If it rained her Dad would insist on giving her a lift. Then she'd have to wait until he'd gone before sneaking off on her own. It really ate into her time when that happened.

Once safely out of sight of watchful parents, Cathy headed away from the Youth Club and into town. A brisk ten-minute walk later and she reached the bright neon oasis of Arcadia, an entertainment complex built just outside the town centre. Here you could find bars, restaurants, cinemas and video arcades.

Cathy's first stop was the public toilets.

She locked herself in a cubicle and took off her clothes. She folded them neatly and swapped them for the clothes contained in her plastic bag. When she left the cubicle she was dressed in cut-off denim shorts, fishnet tights, a black bra and a denim waistcoat, with black knee-length boots to complete the transformation. She never dared to put on any make-up, although she dearly longed to, because she could never be sure she'd have enough time to wash it off properly, and sometimes her Dad was waiting up for her when she got home. She made up for it by wearing cheap, gaudy jewellery, rings, bracelets and necklaces.

Happy with her new look, Cathy strode purposefully towards The Arena, a state-of-the-art video arcade that also housed common-or-garden pinball machines and pool tables. That wasn't what drew Cathy. The lure for her was in the clientele. Or rather, one punter in particular.

Zeke.

God, the very thought of him made her go weak at the knees. He was awesome! Big and strong and dirty, just like a man should be. He had the most bitchin' tattoo across his forehead. HATE, it said. That really summed it up in Cathy's view. One day she was going to be his woman. Oh sure, he already had two women, Mags and Dee, but they were old, at least twenty-four or twenty-five, and so ugly! It was just a matter of time before Cathy replaced both of them. Naturally, she wasn't going to share him. She just knew that when Zeke found out how good she could make him feel, he'd kick those two old bags out of his bed like they had leprosy!

Cathy was still a bit hazy on exactly how she'd make Zeke feel that good. She knew all about sex, of course. I mean, who doesn't, right? It was just that she was a little short on practical experience, that's all. Not that it mattered, she told herself. Zeke would appreciate her freshness and enthusiasm, and he'd show her how to please him. And Cathy would do whatever he asked.

'Cathy!'

She jerked her head in the direction of the voice, her heart pounding guiltily.

Oh Christ! What if someone's recognised me? What if it's a friend of my mother's? I'll die! Would they believe I was going to a costume party?

And then she saw the owner of the voice rushing towards her.

Colin!

She groaned. Not him. Not now. Colin had been in the fifth year when she was in the first year at Westbourne College. He was a nerd, a prat, a long streak of dullness in a khaki anorak. He'd fallen madly in love with her from the first time he set eyes on her. He'd sent her poems, flowers, chocolates, and even after he left school he used to follow her around, gazing at her adoringly.

All in all, he was the most excruciatingly embarrassing experience of Cathy's young life.

What if Zeke sees me with him? I'll die!

Cathy strode quickly towards The Arena. It looked like a dark, noisy cave. If she could just get inside she knew she would be safe. It looked busy tonight. Somewhere in there Zeke was waiting; Cathy could feel his presence.

'Cathy!' This time the voice was right next to her ear. Colin grabbed her arm. She jerked it away angrily.

'Hey!' she said. 'Don't handle the merchandise if you can't afford to buy it!'

God, that sounded tough! Real biker talk.

Colin looked a little bemused, but then, that was his natural expression. He was breathing heavily and his face was flushed.

'Cathy,' he panted. 'Thank God I'm in time.'

'In time for what, Colin?'

'To save you.'

'Save me from what?'

'From "them".' Colin's voice dropped to a conspiratorial whisper. 'The Devil's henchmen.'

Cathy laughed. 'This time, Colin,' she told him, 'you have definitely flipped.'

She started to push past him, but he barred her way.

'It's true,' he said. 'You can't see it, because they have a mesmeric hold over you.'

'Bullshit, Colin! Get out of my way.'

Cathy was getting angry now and a little frightened. Even Colin had never been this weird before! People were starting to stare.

'It's true, Cathy,' Colin persisted. 'Even you must see that this is not the real you. Just look at the way you're dressed.'

Cathy stuck her hands on her hips and thrust out her chest.

'What's wrong with the way I look?' she asked, defiantly.

'It's lewd!' Colin replied. 'The way you expose yourself for all to see, when you should be saving yourself for someone special.'

Cathy grinned. 'In other words,' she said, 'this turns you on. Right, Colin?'

Colin blushed and Cathy laughed.

'That's what this is all about, isn't it?' she continued. 'You like looking at me dressed like this, but you're pissed off because I don't fancy you. Right?'

'No,' Colin protested. 'My own feelings don't come into this!'

'Oh yeah?' Cathy shot out her hand, reaching under the hem of Colin's anorak and up between his thighs. Colin shouted and jumped back.

'Oh, wow!' Cathy laughed, delighted. 'Is that a gun in your pocket, or are you just pleased to see me, big boy?'

Colin blushed furiously. 'That's the devil in you,' he shouted. 'If you won't listen to me, then listen to the words of the one, true God!'

Colin fumbled in his pocket and pulled out a transistor radio. Frantically he began twiddling the knobs, but the radio remained stubbornly silent.

Cathy shook her head. 'Colin,' she said, 'you need treatment.'

As she moved past him, he shot out his hand once more and grabbed her arm tightly. 'This is his instrument!' he bellowed, 'and you will listen!'

Cathy struggled to pull away, but this time his grip was too strong.

'Let go of me, you bastard!' she shouted.

'I am your saviour!' Colin screamed.

'Maybe she don't wanna be saved.'

This was a new voice, deep and rough. Cathy's heart missed a beat. Zeke!

A small crowd had gathered to watch the altercation, but they parted like the Red Sea as Zeke pushed his way through to the front. He had two other bikers with him: a short, shaven-headed man with a bushy beard who went by the name of Weasel, and a tall Nordic blonde with a body-builder's physique, called Karl.

'He's just like my knight in shining armour,' Cathy thought, 'come to rescue me!'

'Zeke!' she called. 'Am I glad to see you!'

Colin thrust out his transistor radio as though it were a cross and Zeke was Bela Lugosi.

'I'm taking her from you,' Colin informed him. 'I will not let you taint this innocent soul!'

'Balls,' said Zeke evenly.

'Let her go, asshole,' Weasel added.

'Or we'll break every bone in your puny body,' Karl finished.

Colin blinked, and thought hard. He prayed for guidance, but found only static on the line. He concluded from this that his deity had no new instructions for him. His mission was clear and he had God on his side; therefore these spawns of Satan could not stop him. A wave of suicidal self-confidence swept over him. He drew himself up to his full height and grinned into the ugly face of death.

'Do your worst!' he challenged. 'I'm taking her out of here and you can't stop me!'

Colin began to back away, dragging the unwilling Cathy with him. Zeke moved closer. Colin brandished his transistor radio.

'Stay back!' he warned.

'Fuck you!' Zeke told him and hit him, just once, in the stomach.

Colin's world went out of focus. He couldn't breathe and none of his limbs felt like they belonged to him.

Cathy took this opportunity to kick him on the shin. He made a choked, gurgling sound and let go of her arm. In a perfect slow-motion swan dive, Colin folded up and fell to his knees. His transistor radio fell from his grasp. Zeke stepped forward, planted one heavily booted heel on the cheap plastic case and ground it into a dozen pieces. Colin watched it happen with the expression of someone who is seeing their only child being torn limb from limb by hungry wolves.

'No!' he whispered. 'No!'

Cathy jumped forward and hugged Zeke's arm to her chest.

'Oh, wow!' she said. 'You were great, Zeke, really great!'

'No problem,' Zeke replied. 'C'mon, let's go,' he instructed. The two bikers and Cathy fell into step with him and headed towards The Arena.

Left behind, Colin crawled forward, sifting the dismembered pieces of his transistor to God through shaking fingers. His whole body began to tremble and a peculiar red mist fell across his eyes. Slowly, painfully, he clambered to his feet. Some twenty feet away his enemy was about to escort Cathy – sweet, innocent, deluded Cathy – through the very gates of Hell. At least, that's how it looked to Colin. Of course, he could not allow that to happen. With an inarticulate roar of rage, Colin launched himself forward.

'Aaaarrrgh!' he screamed, and leapt the last six feet to land on Zeke's back, his arms windmilling punches onto the biker's head and shoulders.

Cathy screamed.

Zeke grunted and staggered forward under the impact. Weasel and Karl moved in quickly, grabbed Colin under the arms and prised him loose. With almost contemptuous ease they threw him away like a bag of rubbish. He landed heavily on his back, and lay there like a beached turtle.

Three menacing shadows circled above him. Weasel and Karl reached down and hauled him to his feet.

Zeke stood in front of him, his face like thunder.

'What shall we do with him, Zeke?' Weasel asked.

An unholy grin split Zeke's face in two.

'Baboon,' he said.

Chapter 15

'Bastard! The evil, slimy, bastard, son of a bitch! I wish he was dead!'

Molly was ranting, screaming and waving her arms. Billy leaned over and whispered in Mike's ear.

'Who's she talking about? Jarvis or you?'

'Sod off,' Mike replied sourly.

Molly's flat was a war zone. Furniture and crockery smashed, clothes ripped to pieces, the Mickey Mouse poster that had brightened her mornings torn from the wall and shredded. Spray paint adorned the walls and ceilings. Even her teddy bear had had his arms and legs cruelly torn off and a carving knife embedded between his eyes. Molly gently eased the knife free, dropped it on the floor and held his poor, dismembered corpse to her ample bosom. Tears began to fill her eyes.

'My mum gave me this bear,' she said softly, her voice breaking as the anger gave way to despair. All I had, she thought, this was all I had, and now it's gone.

'Look on the bright side,' Mike suggested.

'What bright side?' Molly asked.

'At least you weren't here when it happened!'

Molly screamed and flew at him, dropping her teddy on the floor in her rage. She lashed out with both hands, catching him resounding slaps about the head, her nails raking his cheek. Mike fell back, raising his hands across his face to protect himself. Molly continued to rain punches and kicks on his arms, legs and shoulders until Billy grabbed her in a bear hug and pulled her off.

'Let me go!' she screamed. 'I'm going to kill him!'

Billy held on grimly, wrestling her onto the bed and falling on top of her.

'He's not worth it, Molly!' he shouted 'He's just not worth it!'

Slowly her struggles ceased. Billy shifted his weight and she turned her tear-stained face towards him.

'This was my home,' she said softly.

'I know, I know.' Billy gently wiped the tears from her cheek. 'But better it than you, eh?'

'What?' Molly sniffed.

'If you'd been here when Jarvis arrived, he'd have done this to you as well as your flat. Maybe, now he's had his fun, he'll leave you alone.'

'Maybe,' Molly admitted, wiping the back of her hand across her face.

Mike dabbed at his gouged cheek with a grubby handkerchief. 'That's what I said!' he complained. 'But when I said it, she went mental!'

'Shut up!' they replied in unison.

Billy helped Molly to her feet.

'Where's Charlie?' she asked suddenly.

All three looked around stupidly, as though expecting him to pop up like a jack-in-the-box from behind the gutted remains of the armchair.

'He was here a minute ago,' Billy said.

'Charlie?' Molly called. 'Charlie, where are you?'

A small knot of fear hardened in her stomach.

If he wanders off now, I may never see him again!

That thought frightened her more than she cared to admit. She pushed past Billy and Mike to check out the devastated kitchen. Apart from scattered cutlery, spoilt food and a paint job consisting of flour, eggs and milk, the room was empty.

'Charlie!' She ran from the kitchen to the bathroom.

He was sitting on the floor, wedged in between the lavatory bowl and the bath, hugging his knees to his chest. His face was hidden between his folded arms. Molly knelt beside him and touched him on the shoulder. Slowly he turned his face towards her. His eyes were red-rimmed, his cheeks wet with tears, his breath sobbing in his throat.

'Charlie,' Molly whispered, 'what's wrong?'

'My fault,' he mumbled. 'All my fault.'

His voice broke and he began to sob, his body shaking convulsively. Molly gathered him up in her arms, hugging him, rocking back and forth, soothing away his fears.

'Hush,' she told him. 'It's all right. It's not your fault. Everything's going to be all right.'

Billy coughed, embarrassed, from the doorway.

'Moll,' he said. 'You can stay at my place tonight, okay?'

'Okay,' she replied. 'Just give me a minute.'

Billy withdrew and left them alone with their tears.

Chapter 16

The smell of turps was making his eyes water.

In a way, Colin was glad of that. It masked the tears of humiliation.

He tipped the bottle and splashed some more of the solvent onto a cloth, then rubbed vigorously at his bare backside.

By standing on the rim of the bath and peering over his shoulder, he could see his rear end reflected in the mirror over the basin.

It was still blue.

He groaned and rubbed again. If only Cathy hadn't been there to see it. If only he could have been spared that ultimate humiliation. Pain he was prepared for. Gladly he would have taken a beating in such a noble cause and worn his scars with pride, but not this. This was too sick for words. It proved, if proof were needed, that these people were depraved beyond all redemption.

Hot tears of rage welled up in his eyes as he played those loathsome events through again in his mind.

They'd dragged him, kicking and screaming, into the games arcade and slammed him, face down, across one of the pinball machines. While two of them held his arms, the third removed his trousers and underpants. Quite a crowd had gathered, all of them laughing and jeering, offering disgusting comments. From this awkward position, Colin couldn't see what happened next, but he heard it. Heard a series of sharp clicks which he later realised was the sound of a spray can being shaken. He heard the crowd roar with laughter. And then he felt it. A fine wet spray across his buttocks and thighs. Back and forth, back and forth. With each pass the crowd roared and clapped their approval even more loudly.

'Degenerates!' Colin had yelled. 'Devil's children. You are corrupt, and you shall pay!'

No one took a blind bit of notice.

Finally their evil work was finished and they took up a chant.

'Baboon-bum, baboon-bum, baboon-bum!'

That most loathsome face, the dark, evil eyes, the tattooed HATE across the forehead, pressed itself close against Colin's own.

'Do you like fruit?' the face asked. A grubby hand appeared, clutching a banana. Then both the face and the hand disappeared, and the chant broke up into gales of unrestrained laughter.

For a second Colin didn't realise what was happening, then his whole body spasmed as the tip of the fruit was pushed between his buttocks. He tried to resist, he ground his teeth, the veins on his forehead standing out like thick, blue cables, and finally he screamed as the banana was rammed home.

Only then did they let him go. Trouserless, humiliated, abused and sobbing, they chased him around the car park, taunting and jeering.

Eventually they grew tired of the chase and let him be.

He was two streets away before he dared to stop and remove the banana. There was blood on the tip.

Fortunately, his anorak was long and the night was dark. Motorists who passed by flashed their lights and sounded their horns. Pedestrians laughed or crossed the street to avoid him.

Luckily, his parents were asleep when he arrived home. He retrieved the turps from the cabinet in the garden shed and locked himself in the bathroom.

This is not the end, he told himself. I will make them all pay for this. The time has come to fight fire with fire.

Chapter 17

'*Sex Slaves From Saturn*? *Wild Willing And Wet*?' Molly read out the titles and stacked the video boxes one on top of the other.

Billy grinned sheepishly. 'My brother owns a video shop,' he explained. 'These are all just free samples. They're not that good really.'

'Don't worry, Billy,' Molly assured him with a small, tired smile. 'Your secret is safe with me.'

Apart from the videos, the room was littered with sheet music, half-read sci-fi novels, guitar cases, tape machines and take-away Chinese food boxes.

'Sorry it's a bit of a mess,' Billy apologised. 'I wasn't expecting company.'

'Compared to my place, this is the Ritz!' Molly commented.

'Yeah, well.' Billy shifted uncomfortably. 'The settee folds down into a bed,' he explained. 'I'll get some pillows and stuff.' He lowered his voice. 'Is Charlie going to be all right?' he asked.

Molly looked across to where Charlie sat, very quietly, on a straight-backed chair, his hands folded loosely in his lap.

'I think so,' she said. 'He's just very sensitive. He was so upset about what happened, you know?'

Billy nodded. 'I'll get those pillows,' he said.

While Billy rummaged in a cupboard, Molly crossed to Charlie's side and put her hand on his shoulder. He looked up at her, his face a mask.

The lights are on, but there's no one home, she thought. Don't back away from me, Charlie, she wanted to shout. Not now, not when I really need someone.

Billy appeared, carrying blankets and pillows. He dumped them onto the settee.

'Okay,' he said. 'I guess I'll turn in.'

'Goodnight, Billy,' Molly said, 'and thanks.'

'No problem. G'night, Charlie.'

Charlie stared at him, but did not reply. Billy shrugged.

'See you in the morning,' he said.

Once Billy had left, Molly busied herself with making up the bed, plumping up pillows and arranging the blankets.

'Hope you don't mind sharing?' she said. 'Billy just kind of assumed we would be. Is that okay with you, Charlie?'

Silence was her only reply. Molly bit her lip.

It's like he's in a trance or something!

Slowly she began to undress. Her fingers fumbled with the buttons.

Boy, she thought, there's a first; I'm actually nervous about taking my clothes off! She looked across at him, but Charlie stared straight ahead, lost in his own world.

When she was naked, Molly crossed the room to stand in front of him.

I wish I was slimmer, she thought. What if he doesn't like me? What if he thinks I'm a tart? What if he's gay?

'Charlie,' she said.

He raised his eyes to hers.

'It's been a hell of a day for both of us,' she said. 'Do you want to go to bed now?'

Somewhere behind his eyes a struggle was going on; she could see it reflected in his eyes. The muscles in his face twitched and jumped, then settled down in a strange fluid ripple that changed his expression from sad to happy and back again. He reached out with both hands, placing his palms flat against the outside of her thighs. Although his touch was warm, the contact made Molly shiver. She gasped as goose-bumps broke out all over her body, but, she decided, it was not unpleasant; in fact, she could get to like his touch very much.

Charlie cleared his throat. He pronounced his words very carefully, as though trying them out for the very first time.

'I think you are very beautiful,' he said.

Molly blushed. 'Oh, Charlie,' she said. 'That's the nicest thing anyone's ever said to me!' And she laughed, gently, as she took his face in her hands and bent to kiss his lips.

At first his mouth was slack, unresponsive. She sensed his hesitation and pulled back.

'What's the matter, Charlie?' she asked. 'Haven't you ever kissed a girl before?'

Charlie struggled to answer. It was important to him that he did.

'Not like this,' he said. 'It didn't feel the same.'

Molly bent forward and kissed him again. This time his mouth moved against hers, his hands slid up her sides and she felt her body tingle. She drew back, panting, and smiled.

'You're a fast learner, Charlie,' she told him. 'Come on, let's go to bed.'

She took him by the hand and he followed her willingly.

Chapter 18

Knock, knock.
Who's there?
The Bad Man.

'No, you can't come in!'
'You can't keep me out, Charlie. The walls have all been knocked down. You have nowhere left to hide.'

Humpty Dumpty.

'I'm coming for you, Charlie.'

Charlie whimpered in his sleep. Molly snuggled closer and murmured 'Poor baby', before returning to her own dream with a smile upon her lips.
Charlie was left alone in the dark.
Alone with his nightmare.
And the Bad Man.

Chapter 19

The telephone rang at 5.37 a.m.

Constance Bannerman muttered darkly and pulled the duvet over her head. It's just part of my dream, she told herself. If I ignore it, it'll go away.

She ignored it, but it didn't go away.

It rang, and rang, and rang.

Whoever it was, was certainly persistent.

With a grunt of frustration, Constance emerged from the duvet like a reluctant snail emerging from its shell. She rolled grudgingly across the cold, empty side of the double bed that she occupied by herself, and picked up the phone. The light from the luminous digital alarm clock guided her hand and informed her, smugly it seemed, of the unearthly hour. She fumbled the handset to her ear.

'What?' she asked, her voice thick with sleep and deep annoyance. She listened to the reply for a few seconds and then said:

'He's not here. Try his fancy piece!'

Then she hung up and rolled back to the warm side of the bed.

Winston George Bannerman.

There was a name to conjure with.

Faced with the monstrous inevitability of being nicknamed 'Winnie', it had been Winston George Bannerman's practice since childhood to insist on being called simply 'Bannerman'. Close friends and lovers were allowed to call him 'B'. It was the only term of affection he would tolerate.

In rare moments of introspection, Bannerman would muse upon the fact that his wife hadn't called him B in years. In fact they rarely communicated at all these days. They had grown apart. Simple as that really. Inertia was the only thing that kept their marriage alive, and even that had started to slip into a decaying orbit lately.

Bannerman allowed Elaine Feathers to call him B. It was, after all, her right as his latest enamorata. He lay beside her, a great mountain of blankets next to her more modest hillock of sheets.

She lay on her back, snoring like a walrus. Something to do with sinus trouble, she maintained. Bannerman wasn't entirely sure if walruses did snore, but they looked like the sort of creatures who did, and if they did he was sure they would sound just like Elaine.

Not that it was the cacophonous reverberations coming from that slim frame that kept him awake. Bannerman had been a martyr to insomnia for many years. It was something he had learned to live with. The job helped, of course, keeping him out till all hours. He was a copper. A Detective Inspector, to be precise. A good one too, by his own modest reckoning. The fact that his file was littered with words like 'stubborn', 'disrespectful' and 'intransigent' didn't worry him unduly. He got results. That's why they tolerated him. When he stopped getting results they'd put him out to grass, but until then he got away with it. Just.

He heard the car pull up outside. Heard the engine die, the door open and close, the creak of the garden gate and the soft footsteps on the path. Then came the discreet knock at the door. Elaine continued with her walrus impression, quite oblivious to her nocturnal visitor.

Bannerman levered his substantial bulk off the mattress and padded across to the window. He pulled back the curtain and opened the window, leaning out into the chilly dawn air to see who was at the door.

The caller looked up, his face a ghostly blur in the half light.

'All right, Rafferty,' Bannerman called jovially, 'I'll come quietly; you can call the dogs off.'

'You weren't at home, sir,' Rafferty replied, a touch peevishly.

'Brilliant deduction, Rafferty. I can see now why they made you a detective,' Bannerman responded.

'But you should have been, sir. You're on call and no one knew where to find you,' Rafferty informed him.

Bannerman sighed. Failure to follow procedures was another comment often repeated in his file.

'You knew where to find me,' he countered. 'Otherwise you wouldn't be here! Now, is there a point to all this, or do you just enjoy waking people up in the middle of the night?'

'There's a job on, sir. You caught the shout.'

'Messy one?'

'Could be, sir.'

Bannerman rubbed his hands. 'Good,' he said. 'I like messy ones. I'll be down in five minutes.'

Bannerman withdrew his head, shut the window and pulled the curtains. Elaine was still snoring loudly. No point in waking her, Bannerman decided, even if I could!

As he padded across the thick pile carpet to where his clothes lay in an untidy heap on a chair, he caught sight of his reflection in the dressing-table mirror. Not a particularly pretty sight, he had to admit, but then he had never intended to grow old gracefully.

Bannerman wasn't yet fifty, but he'd never see forty again. Bit like my waistline, he mused to himself as he dressed.

He didn't bother to leave a note to explain his absence. When you're someone's bit-on-the-side, especially a copper's bit-on-the-side, you get used to waking up alone.

Ten minutes after the tentative knock on his mistress's door, Bannerman was sitting beside Rafferty as they sped through the sparse early morning traffic towards the centre of town.

'Where are we going?' Bannerman asked.

'Video Dome, sir,' Rafferty replied.

Bannerman grunted. 'That cesspit,' he said. 'Only a matter of time before they made the jump to a major nasty. What is it, an over-enthusiastic bouncer caught someone an unfortunate one with a baseball bat?'

'No, sir. It's the owner, a Mr Jarvis. He's been stabbed to death.'

'Well, Rafferty,' said Bannerman, eyeing the mortal remains of Richard Alexander Jarvis, 'I didn't know you were such a master of understatement.'

Rafferty stood beside him, slowly going green and rocking gently to and fro. 'I hadn't viewed the scene, sir,' he said in a small, tight voice. 'The call just indicated a fatality involving a knife.'

Bannerman nodded. 'Accurate enough,' he conceded, 'but a bit prosaic to describe all this, wouldn't you say?'

Rafferty nodded. At the moment he didn't feel like saying anything at all. In fact, the tighter he could keep his mouth shut, the better he would like it.

'All right, Rafferty,' Bannerman said generously, 'wait for me outside.'

'Yes, sir,' mumbled Rafferty gratefully, and almost ran from the room.

Rafferty was a good lad, Bannerman decided, but he still had a lot to learn. Bit paranoid about doing things by the book. And if he was going to stay in this line of work, he'd do well to develop a stronger constitution. Mind you, this little job would test the strongest of stomachs.

Bannerman felt no remorse at the passing of Slick Rick Jarvis. The man was a pimp, a pusher and a pornographer. The room where he met his end was testimony enough to the sort of profession he was in. Furnished with a bed, a camera and lighting rig, the walls held various whips, restraints and other appliances that Bannerman didn't even want to guess as to their purpose.

Even so, no one really deserved to die the way Jarvis had.

The deceased was naked, tied spreadeagled to the bed. His blood had sprayed the walls and saturated the mattress, and now dripped into several congealing pools on the floor. A gag had been forced into Jarvis's mouth, and from the look on his face he had taken a long time to die. Bits of him, fingers, ears, toes and genitals, had been hacked off and arranged neatly about the corpse. Dozens of knife wounds were evident on his arms, legs and chest. Macabre enough, but the final touch were the words scrawled upon the wall in the victim's own blood. Just four words in ragged, crimson capitals.

DO YOU PLAY CHESS?

Bannerman studied those words for several seconds, until it became obvious that his presence was hampering the work of the crime lab people, who were swarming over the scene with their plastic gloves and tweezers. Bannerman turned once more to the corpse.

'Don't worry, old son,' he told him. 'I'll find the little toe-rag who did this to you and give him a severe talking to.'

Bannerman removed himself from the scene of the crime, and found Rafferty lurking in the corridor looking ashen-faced but stoic.

'Who found the body?' Bannerman asked.

'Bobby on the beat, sir,' Rafferty replied. 'Saw the back door wide open. When he investigated he found this little lot.'

'Score one for the boys in blue,' said Bannerman. 'I'll need to talk to him later. In the meantime, round up everyone who's worked in this palace of delights in the last six months. Especially those who were here last night. I want them to give us a list of every punter who came through that door.'

'That could be hundreds of people, sir! You can't mean you want to question all of them!'

'Of course I don't, Sergeant. That's your job.'

Rafferty's face fell.

'Well, get on with it,' Bannerman told him.

'Yes, sir,' said Rafferty, resignedly. 'Where will you be if I need you, sir?'

'I'll be in Records,' Bannerman replied. 'Looking up an old friend.'

It was the sound of splashing water that drew Molly from sleep. She stretched and yawned. Her hand reached out and encountered empty space where there should have been warm flesh. For a second she panicked, and then realised the significance of the splashing water.

He's only taking a shower; don't get so paranoid, she told herself.

Molly lay back and scolded herself for being so stupid. He's not going to walk out on you now, she told herself. Not after last night, anyhow! She'd wait for him to finish his shower and then make breakfast, she decided. Then they'd both go out and start their lives all over again.

Five minutes later the shower was still running. A small, nagging voice in her mind told her something was wrong. Molly got out of bed and tiptoed across to the bathroom door. She knocked softly.

'Charlie?' she called. 'Are you all right in there?'

When she received no reply, she tried the door. It was open. She stepped inside. The shower curtain was drawn around the bath. With pounding heart she drew it back.

'Charlie,' she whispered, 'what's wrong?'

He was sitting with his knees drawn up, at one end of the bath, the spray from the shower hitting his head and shoulders. Molly reached out her hand and then drew it back with a gasp.

The water was turning into a fine pink froth as it gurgled away down the plughole, but there was no mistaking the dark stains on Charlie's arms and hands.

Blood.

Chapter 20

Elephants and Bannerman.

Neither of them ever forget. There are, of course, other similarities. Both are big, grey and wrinkled, but it was their common capacity to remember that sent Bannerman scurrying to the vaults to delve back through the files.

It was the summer of 1969 when Chess cast his shadow across the city. Bannerman had just joined the force, a brand new PC straight out of the box with his very first pointy hat, when Chess made his mark.

Chess was not your usual serial killer. Most victims of that sort of crime fall into the same category. Prostitutes, gays, vagrants, whatever type the perpetrator feels has offended him, but there's always a common link.

Not with Chess. His victims had no discernible connection. They were different sexes, came from different backgrounds, had no known associations in common.

The only thing that linked them was the way they died. Always with a knife. Always in the victim's own home, with no sign of forced entry. Always savage mutilation.

Just like the Jarvis killing.

No. Not quite the same. Something was missing. In 1969 Chess always marked his kills by leaving a white pawn from a chess set on the victim. That's how the press had come to call him the Chess Killer.

No such pawn was found on Jarvis, but the message, scrawled in blood on the wall, had been enough to send chills down Bannerman's spine.

Chess had been a cocky bastard. Not content with slaughtering three people, he had taunted the police with little notes after each kill. The notes were always the same. DO YOU PLAY CHESS? Always in the victim's blood. This particularly nasty habit had been kept back from public consumption. Nobody knew about it except the killer and the police.

And now, there it was, twenty-four years later, scrawled across Rick Jarvis's wall.

In 1969 the killings just stopped, as suddenly as they had begun. Public interest moved on to other atrocities and resources were gradually redirected, but the case never closed. Bannerman never forgot. Bannerman and elephants. Not that he'd been closely involved in the case all those years ago, but he had been there when one of the bodies was discovered. He'd thrown up all over his nice new shiny boots. For that, if nothing else, Chess owed him one.

That's why Bannerman found himself sitting in an uncomfortable chair, leafing through old files, making notes as he read.

Is it you? he asked himself. How can it be? he argued. This was over twenty-four years ago; you'd be older than Methuselah by now! Or would you? I'm still here, older, heavier, craftier, so why not you? But what have you been doing in the meantime?

Bannerman's musings were cut short by the sharp clatter of the main door being flung open, followed by the urgent sound of running footsteps.

Rafferty appeared at his side, breathless and red-faced.

'Sir,' he panted, 'we've got him!'

'Got who?'

'Jarvis's killer.'

'What?' Bannerman shot to his feet, galvanised, knocking over his chair in his haste.

'Well, we haven't pulled him in yet,' Rafferty explained, 'but we know who he is.'

'So, are you going to tell me, or do I have to play twenty bloody questions?' Bannerman exploded.

'Sorry, sir. His name's Stevey Johnston, a known associate of Jarvis.'

'And what makes you think he's the culprit?'

'You remember that camera, sir? The one in the room where Jarvis was killed?'

Bannerman nodded. 'Yes, yes,' he said. 'Get on with it!'

'When they took it to the lab, they found a film in it. The killer, Johnston, had filmed the whole thing!'

Chapter 21

Stevey Johnston hadn't been hard to find.

The hard part had been watching him butcher Rick Jarvis.

When the tape began, it was focused on the empty bed. Johnston walked into shot, carrying the unconscious Jarvis over his shoulder like a sack of potatoes. Both men were naked. Johnston threw Jarvis onto the bed, tied him down and gagged him. Then he slapped him around the face until he regained consciousness.

Johnston walked off-camera. When he reappeared he was carrying a knife. Before starting his grisly work he paused to grin into the camera, a perfect mug shot, as though he wanted to make sure he was recognised. Then he turned back to the bed and began to cut.

They arrested Johnston at 10.30 that morning.

By midday Bannerman was fuming.

'Who the hell broke his arms?' he demanded.

'It wasn't my lads,' the duty sergeant informed him. 'Says he was attacked, night before last, him and Jarvis both.'

'The hospital confirms it, sir,' Rafferty chipped in. 'Johnston and Jarvis were treated for broken bones, cuts and bruises. Neither would say how it happened.'

'Bad breaks, are they?' Bannerman asked.

'Pretty bad, sir.'

'Bad enough to stop him carting a full-grown man about like a kiddie's toy and then carving him into little pieces, are they?'

'Well, I'm no medical expert, sir, but I'd say so, yes.'

'Oh, you would, would you?' Bannerman fumed. 'Then, in that case, who the hell was that sodding maniac we saw on the tape?'

Bannerman let the question hang in the air as he stormed off to speak with the prisoner.

Molly was worried as hell.

She'd heard of people who bled for no reason, but that was supposed to be a religious experience.

Molly knew she was good in bed, but she'd hardly call it a religious experience!

But what else could it be?

Charlie had no cuts or scratches anywhere on his entire body. A nosebleed then? Hardly likely, but what else?

Charlie couldn't even remember starting to bleed, or getting into

74

the shower for that matter. The tears and the trauma of yesterday seemed to have washed away from him with the stains on his hands. He was in a good mood, like a little kid going on holiday; he was looking forward to the rehearsal. Molly didn't like to bring him down, so she pushed the fears to the back of her mind, but they refused to stay there. They'd sneak out every now and then and gnaw at her like hungry rats.

He's not sick.

He's not insane.

He's not a religious fanatic.

She kept repeating her litany of 'He's nots' to herself to drive the rat-fears away. They would pretend to retreat, then poke their nasty little snouts back around the corner and shout:

'If you're so smart, tell us what he is, not what he's not.'

Molly had no answer for that and the rat-fears would snigger behind their paws and creep a bit closer.

'Screw you,' she muttered. 'He's just confused, that's all.'

Molly watched him now, as Billy taught him some chords on the keyboard.

'Am I in love with you?' she asked herself.

The rat-fears really tore into that one, so she stopped thinking and began to tidy up the rehearsal room, just to keep her mind occupied. The bunker where they rehearsed had been an old MOD communications centre during the war. It was disused now, but its thick concrete walls made it completely soundproof and an ideal place to practise without disturbing the neighbours. To make it even more perfect, it was situated at the bottom of Billy's grandmother's garden, so they got to use it for free.

'You'll have to move out if there's another war,' the old lady told them, 'because that's when they'll want it back.'

They had promised faithfully to vacate the premises as soon as hostilities were declared, and the old lady had gone away quite happy.

Now, they were waiting for Mike to turn up. He was late as usual.

'Where the hell is he?' Molly complained.

As if on cue the door opened and Mike walked in.

'I've got some good news and some bad news,' he announced. 'Which do you want first?'

'The bad,' Molly replied. 'Knowing you, the good news will be even worse!'

Mike scowled at her. 'Okay,' he said, 'the bad news is that the chip shop didn't have any sausages in batter, so I had to get cod instead.' He placed a greasy paper bundle on top of one of the amps.

'S'okay,' said Billy, 'fish is good for the brain, anyway. What's the good news?'

'Oh, that!' Mike paused for dramatic effect. 'Rick Jarvis is dead,' he said.

Dr Elizabeth Barrett was used to strange requests, especially if it involved a police case, but somehow, whenever Inspector Bannerman was involved the requests seemed stranger than usual. Bannerman was waiting for her as soon as she stepped through the door.

'Dr Barrett,' he greeted her. 'So good of you to come so quickly. This shouldn't take long. If you'd like to follow me.'

Bannerman led her off at a brisk pace to an interview room.

'If you could just give me some idea what this is all about, Inspector,' Dr Barrett protested. 'Your message was very vague.'

'I do apologise, Dr Barrett, but for security reasons I had to be discreet. Do sit down.'

Bannerman closed the door behind them and pulled up a chair for himself.

'I want you to examine a suspect,' he said.

'Is he injured?' the doctor asked.

'He's got two broken arms,' Bannerman confirmed, 'but that's not why I want you to take a look at him.'

'Then why do you want me to see him?' she asked, exasperated.

'All in good time, Dr Barrett, all in good time. There's something I'd like you to do first.'

'What's that?'

'I'd like you to look at these pictures of naked men!'

'I wish he were dead!'

That's what I said, and now he is! And Charlie woke up with blood on his hands! Molly's thoughts were spinning crazily. That's ridiculous, she told herself. Charlie couldn't have had anything to do with Jarvis's death. Could he? Maybe he's a genie, she thought. That's why he can't remember anything. He's a genie who's been sent to earth as some sort of punishment to do the bidding of the first person who shows him any kindness. Me! And when I wished Jarvis dead, bingo! Charlie the Genie got the job done! Maybe I should turn myself in right away. I can just hear the charges being read out:

'You are hereby accused of wilful wishing and possession of an unlawful genie. How do you plead?'

Guilty, but insane. That's how I should plead!

Molly sighed and looked again at the early edition of the local paper that Mike had brought with him.

Jarvis had made headline news, but details were vague. The stop press said that someone was helping the police with their inquiries, so that was encouraging. It has nothing to do with you, she told herself, so stop worrying; no one else is.

That much was certainly true. After an initial flurry of interest, the topic was dropped, relegated to the 'good riddance to bad rubbish' pile and forgotten about.

The rest of the afternoon was spent going through Elvis's Greatest Hits. Mike would play the tape so that Charlie could get the right inflection and Charlie would duplicate it, note for note. It was almost too easy, but Charlie seemed to be having great fun. Molly was pleased about that, at least. He didn't strike her as the sort who had a great deal of fun in his life. Somehow, though, she just couldn't bring herself to join in the happy mood, and sat most of the numbers out. Billy would have to go through the bass lines with her later anyway, and there really wasn't much for her to do except sit and brood.

She listened to them run through 'Way Down' for the umpteenth time. Each time they would fall about at the way Charlie would get that basement-deep note right at the end. Molly guessed it was pretty funny at that. Such a deep, graveyard sound coming from such an unlikely source.

'Jesus!' Billy laughed. 'You are gonna knock 'em dead, believe me.'

Charlie smiled, pleased as punch.

'If only he looked more like Elvis,' Mike said. 'I suppose we could get a wig, maybe some platform shoes or something. What do you think?'

Charlie frowned. 'Don't you like the way I look?' he asked.

'Hey, don't get me wrong, Charlie,' Mike explained. 'There's nothing wrong with the way you look, as such. It's just that you're supposed to look like Elvis.'

Charlie picked up the cassette they had been listening to all afternoon and stared at the picture on the cover. It showed Elvis in his GI days, all crewcut and tanned.

'You mean you want me to look like this?' he asked.

Mike was getting a little exasperated now. 'That would be nice, yes,' he said.

'Hey!' Molly said, 'don't have a go at Charlie. It's not his fault.'

'I'm not having a go at anyone!' Mike protested. 'All I'm saying is...'

Billy's shout stopped Mike in mid-sentence. At first it looked like Charlie was having a fit. His face was jerking and twitching, and then it seemed to melt, the bones moving beneath the skin, the skin itself changing colour. But the weirdest thing was his hair. It shrank. Just pulled back into his scalp and darkened from its natural mousy colour to jet black.

Molly couldn't breathe; her legs felt like they were about to give way. She'd heard of people who were caught in powerful bomb blasts having their skin literally melted off, but she never thought she'd see it for real. Except it wasn't really melting, it was changing, rearranging, becoming something else.

When the changes finally stopped, Charlie had ceased to exist. Elvis Aaron Presley had taken his place, identical in every way to the picture on the cassette cover.

'Is this how I'm supposed to look?' he asked in Charlie's voice.

Mike Menagerie fainted dead away.

Stevey Johnston was scared to death.

Rick was dead and he stood to go down for it. But that was ridiculous! He'd had nothing to do with it. How could he anyway, with two broken arms?

That fat bastard, Bannerman, said they had proof. There couldn't be, unless someone had gone to a lot of trouble to set him up. But who would hate him enough to do something like that?

Stevey stopped counting when the list of names numbered more than twenty; it was too depressing. He shivered and pulled the blanket closer around his shoulders. All his clothes had been taken for examination. That didn't cheer him up either. They could do all sorts of things these days. If he'd so much as sneezed in Rick's presence within the last month, it would be enough to put him at the scene of the crime.

A key jangled in the lock and the cell door swung open.

Bannerman bustled in, followed by an efficient-looking woman in her mid-fifties.

'Where's your manners?' Bannerman asked. 'Stand up when a lady enters the room.'

Stevey stood up.

'Good,' said Bannerman. 'Now, drop the blanket so we can have a good look at you.'

Stevey stared at him blankly. 'I've got nothing on under here,' he told him.

'So?' Bannerman replied flatly.

'She's a woman,' Stevey explained.

'Full marks. Won't need to test his eyesight now, will we, Doctor?'

'A doctor? Is that true?' Stevey asked.

'Yes, she's a doctor, but if she was a butcher she'd have seen better looking carcasses than yours hanging up in her shop window! Now, stop being coy and get rid of the blanket.'

'Young man, I am a bona fide medical practitioner,' Dr Barrett confirmed, 'and if you would just do as the Inspector asks we can get this charade over and done with.'

Reluctantly, Stevey let the blanket fall to the ground.

Dr Barrett took a slow walk all the way around him, scrutinising carefully.

'Very well,' she said at last. 'I've seen enough.'

'And I've seen more than enough!' Bannerman added. 'All right, sunshine, cover yourself up before you frighten the horses!'

'Does it hurt?'

'How did you do that?'

'Can you do anyone?'

'How did you do that?'

'Can you teach me how to do it?'

'How did you do that?'

'Can you turn into animals as well?'

'HOW THE FUCKING HELL DID YOU DO THAT?'

Mike looked like he was about to explode; the force of his shout felt like it had shredded his vocal cords.

Charlie shrugged. 'I don't know how I do it,' he answered. 'I think I was born that way.'

'We have to think,' Mike croaked. 'I mean, this is a whole new ball-game. The potential here is not just big, it's huge, it's mega, it's . . . bloody brilliant!' He collapsed, exhausted, into an old deckchair. A slow, dreamy smile crossed his face.

'I've seen that look before,' Billy said.

'So have I,' Molly agreed. 'He's dreaming about money.'

Bannerman sat across from Dr Barrett in one of the interview rooms. The photos he had shown her earlier were spread out in front of her.

'So,' he asked, 'in your opinion, Doctor, is the man in these photos the same person that you saw in the cell?'

Dr Barrett picked up the photos one by one and studied them again. They were stills taken from the video of Jarvis's murder. Each one showed someone who seemed to be Stevey Johnston. Full face, side face, full frontal, back view.

'It's very difficult to make any sort of judgement on this sort of evidence,' she said, 'but facially there's a remarkable similarity.'

'Are they the same person?' Bannerman pushed.

She shook her head. 'I'd have to say no. It's not a medical opinion, you understand. Any layman can see the difference.'

'Even so, Doctor, perhaps you could amplify, just a bit?'

'Well,' she began, 'apart from the very obvious fact that the specimen you have in the cells has two broken arms, he is also scrawny, with poor muscle tone and posture. Whereas this man,' she tapped the photo, 'has a well-defined physique and an altogether huskier build.'

'Is there any type of drug, a steroid perhaps, that could have brought about this type of short-term physical change?' Bannerman asked.

'That's an absurd notion, Inspector. If you even suggest it in a court of law you deserve to have your case thrown out, there and then.'

Bannerman sighed. 'Could they be twins?' he asked.

'Possible. But there's no way to prove it on this evidence. Now, I really must be going. Is there anything else I can do for you, Inspector?'

'No, thank you,' he replied grimly. 'You've done more than enough already.'

Chapter 22

What's that smell?

It's the midnight oil burning.

It was three in the morning before Bannerman closed the file he was reading and growled:

'Got the bastard!'

Until then it had been a thankless day. They'd had to release Johnston, which hadn't gone down at all well with anyone, but there really was no other choice. At least six people swore blind that Johnston had spent the evening with them until gone one, at some party or other miles away. Add to that the physical differences between Johnston and whoever it was with his face carving up Jarvis on film, and there really didn't seem much point in holding on to him. Johnston had some crazy story about some runaway he'd picked up who'd broken his arms and smashed Jarvis's face, but when it came down to it he couldn't describe him, didn't know his name, where he was now, or where he came from! Bannerman was more inclined to put the injuries down to a lovers' tiff between the two of them and leave it at that.

Plenty of police manpower was being used taking statements and running down leads, but it was all leading precisely nowhere.

Bannerman was convinced that the real key to all this lay in 1969. He'd spent most of the day poring over the old files again and again, until he felt as if his eyeballs would drop out.

I'm missing something, he kept telling himself.

But what?

Three victims.

The first, Roger Delaney, forty-three, single, an antiques dealer and a known, but discreet, homosexual. Killed on June 6th.

The second, Laura Matherson, thirty-one, divorced, American, worked on a fashion magazine. Killed on July 14th.

The third, Debbie Trent, nineteen, single, part-time model, part-time hippie. Killed on August 20th.

None of the victims knew each other; they all had different backgrounds; no common denominator at all.

I'm missing something!

Bannerman read doggedly through the mountain of paperwork. Scrutinised the statements taken from every friend, relation, colleague of the three victims.

Something's missing, but what?

And then he paused. His fingers trembled slightly as he flicked back through the papers, checking and cross-checking.

Of course! The missing pattern was staring him right in the face. It seemed so obvious now, but at the time it could easily have been over-looked.

In any case of this size it takes time to trace all the known associates of the victims. Sometimes you never do find all of them. If the case is solved, it doesn't matter. If the case remains unsolved, but resources are redeployed, no one ever follows it up. It was the same in 1969. There were several names, friends, contacts, acquaintances of each victim who were never interviewed. People who were hanging around the periphery of their lives, with no address, no background. No name was common to all three victims, but if you looked carefully one name in each case stuck out a mile.

Jeffery Bishop.

Lawrence King.

Marcus Knight.

Bishop. King. Knight.

All pieces on a chessboard!

All the same man?

He was toying with us all the time, Bannerman told himself. Flaunt-ing himself right under our noses!

That was when Bannerman closed the file and said:

'Got the bastard!'

Chapter 23

He decided to take the tube.

It was the commuter rush. Crowded. Just the way he liked it. Ideal for window shopping.

Payne found his way into a corner seat, closed his eyes and opened his mind. A psychic pickpocket, he dipped into thoughts, sampling, testing and moving on. His fellow men never ceased to amaze him with their diversity. Sitting there with their folded arms, Walkmans clamped tight, eyes closed or fixed on newspaper or book. Keep Out, the signs said, I'm an individual, don't crowd my space, don't dare to assume that because we share this same high-speed sardine can, that I wish to know anything about you, and I certainly won't let you know anything about me!

If only they knew how much I already know! he mused. For instance: a mousy woman in the corner was a murderer. No question. She had killed her own mother. Smothered her with a pillow when she could take the old woman's nagging no more.

A respectable solicitor in his pin-striped suit was secretly a flasher who exposed himself to schoolgirls.

A young woman was pregnant by someone other than her husband. Someone who was a different colour to her husband! Hard to explain when the baby is born.

The usual round of petty thieves and moral aberrations.

And one gem. A mind like his own. No, perhaps not that exactly. He'd never found a mind quite like his own, but this one was certainly not the norm. It knew it was being spied upon. It resented it. 'Go away!' it screamed. 'Keep out of my mind or I'll hurt you!' Payne didn't take the threat seriously. It was a reflex action, a mental tape loop; the individual didn't even know it was happening, not consciously. He'd encountered many like this. The barriers were there for a reason. It could be mental discipline or mental aberration. He could break down the barriers. Take a psychic axe to those mental doors. He'd done so lots of times before. Sometimes for payment, sometimes for pleasure. Sonia had been for pleasure. Hers as well as his. She was unusual; she knew the barriers were there and wanted them removed. It hurt, but she wanted it to hurt, wanted to see what lay behind those closed portals in her head. This one didn't want to know. Payne didn't have the time or the curiosity to probe deeper. He rattled the door and let it go.

He opened his eyes. His telepathic jog had left him refreshed and invigorated. Like wearing someone else's cast-offs. He soaked up the left-over vibrations, clothed himself in their dreams, wore their lives on his back. It charged his batteries, compensated for the damped-down feeling the pills generated. He needed the pills, of course. Otherwise the input of raw vibrations would swamp him. As he grew older, more experienced, he needed the pills less and less. And when he was on an assignment he didn't need them at all.

He brought his mind back to his current task.

Charlatan.

Such an intriguing case. His physical ability was as remarkable in its own way as Payne's mental skills, but his mind, alas, was definitely below par. His short-term memory was good, but long-term was patchy. By nature he was compliant, childlike, trusting, sometimes acutely inci-sive. He could be taught; in fact, he picked up things very quickly, but forgot them just as fast. Abandoned at birth by some poor cow who thought she'd given birth to a Martian, he was lucky to be talent spot-ted by Warlord, otherwise he might not have survived. Warlord knew how to nurture such a rare talent; he'd had practice. Charlatan, how-ever, was tricky, his usefulness strictly limited until Payne was assigned to his case. All it took was the right programming, really. Much like a trained dog, he could be taught to do tricks, to sit up and beg, to die for the Queen, to kill for your master. He still needed close control in the field, of course, and for the last three years Payne and Charlatan had been a veritable double act. And then Charlatan changed. He did-n't want to play any more. Barriers came up inside his mind. Barriers that even Payne found increasingly difficult to break down. For some-one so pliant the change was really quite remarkable. Payne knew he would succeed, of course. It was just a matter of time and tactics. Of knowing how hard to push.

Except now someone had pushed him over the edge.

Payne sighed. He really hoped he wouldn't have to kill Charlatan. They were similar in so many ways. Granted, Payne had been twenty before being institutionalised. For his own good, they told him at the time. It was probably true. Before that Payne had been a wild youth. A very, very bad boy.

It was Warlord who had really saved him. Recognised his potential, trained him, nurtured him, made sure the boffins perfected the drug, affectionately known as Olympian Blue, to keep his power in check. In many ways Warlord had been like a father to him, far more than his own father anyway.

Morgan Payne's wife had died giving birth to their son. Morgan tried not to hold it against the child, but remained aloof and distant, letting the boy run wild. A wealthy man, his position as head of a pharma-ceutical company had enabled him to provide the prototype for

Olympian Blue when his son started to develop strange mental aber-rations in his teens. He had no idea, of course, what the real problem was, and the drug in that form was not nearly as effective as it should have been. Even so it was, perhaps, his most important contribution to his son's upbringing.

Morgan Payne had died of a heart attack when Harry was twenty. Or so they thought. No one knew about the blazing row between father and son that had triggered off the seizure that claimed Morgan Payne's life. To this day Harry was not sure if he actually caused his father's death or not. It was not something which bothered him either way.

In those days Warlord had simply been 'Uncle Joe', a friend of his father's who was 'something in Whitehall'. When things began to get really out of hand, Uncle Joe had visited Harry and made him an offer he just couldn't refuse. Warlord looked after him from that day on. More, he understood him. Certainly he used him, but Payne never held that against him; he was enjoying himself too much. In his time he had been an interrogator, a debriefer, a mole and an assassin. All under Warlord's watchful eye and careful tutelage. He had excelled in every role.

Now, it seemed, he was to be a hunter, but at least he now knew where to start looking.

DO YOU PLAY CHESS?

It stood out like a beacon.

The police, of course, had not released that bit of information to the general public, but it was in the copy of the report that had found its way across Payne's desk earlier that day.

He had him now.

A general location anyway.

I wonder what triggered the response this time? he mused.

Not that it mattered. The target was now sighted. It was just a mat-ter of time.

Chapter 24

Chief Superintendent Piggott's ulcer was giving him gyp.

He belched loudly, but it did little to relieve the discomfort.

Some people, he knew, grew quite fond of their ulcers and even gave them names. Chief Superintendent Piggott was not the sort of man to give an ulcer a name. Had he been that sort of man, he would probably have called his ulcer Winston George Bannerman.

'Why me, Lord?' he asked, but the Almighty declined to answer. On the face of it, there was an open and shut case that not even Bannerman could foul up. The killer had filmed himself in the act, for Heaven's sake!

And then everything started to go wrong.

I should have guessed, Piggott told himself. Nothing Bannerman does is ever straightforward. It's a law of nature. Like shit always flows downhill. And when it does, it always ends up all over Bannerman!

And now this. The final straw. An urgent fax from Whitehall, approved by the Commissioner himself, no less. Some 'spook' called Payne was on his way down here to start meddling. Piggott hated spooks, spies, secret service, call them what you like. A more supercilious, underhanded bunch of double-dealing little snakes you couldn't wish to meet. James Bond? He wouldn't last two minutes out on a beat. Well, Piggott promised himself, Bannerman's in charge of this case, so he can bloody well baby-sit, not me!

The Warren Street station was in uproar as Piggott left his office.

Dozens of people, patrons and employees of Video Dome, lined the corridors, waiting to give evidence. Piggott snarled. Another of Bannerman's bright ideas! He pushed his way through the milling throng and burst like a summer storm into Bannerman's office. It was disappointingly empty.

'Typical,' Piggott muttered. 'Causes chaos, then buggers off!'

Piggott crossed to the cluttered desk, travelling more in hope than in expectation, and picked up Bannerman's diary. He flicked through the pages until he came to today's date.

The entry was just two words long.

'Gone Fishing,' it said.

Piggott belched painfully and left the room.

Chapter 25

She was waiting for him.

Curled up on the doorstep like yesterday's milk bottle. Payne knew she'd be there. He'd sensed her more than an hour ago. Remarkable really, hers was such a small talent compared to his own. Desperation must have made her push herself to the limits, sending out her telepathic messengers to call him. Funny how they always took the form of shadowy birds. Dark and insubstantial they were, half glimpsed out of the corner of your eyes, then disappearing, no matter how quickly you turned around to confront them. Everyone had them in one form or another. Most people were incapable of using them, that particular door to knowledge forever welded shut. Even Payne had never mastered that particular art, whereas Sonia was actually quite adept, but then, he smiled to himself, she had a good teacher. They were flocking now, her messengers, overflying his path, perching on the railings that led down to his flat.

She sat on the dirty concrete, her legs drawn up to her chin, eyes hollow and dark-rimmed, chewing on a fingernail already chewed to the quick. As he appeared at the top of the steps and looked down at her, she scrambled to her feet, smiling nervously, licking her lips, as though in anticipation of a feast.

'I knew you were coming,' she told him. 'I sensed it.'

Payne brushed past her and put a key into the lock.

'I live here,' he told her. 'I was bound to turn up sooner or later. You don't need to be psychic to work that one out.'

Sonia ignored the rebuff and followed him inside. She looked as though she hadn't eaten in days. The flat had been cleaned and tidied since her last visit. Everything was neat and sparkling, almost military in its precision. Payne himself was almost unrecognisable as the unshaven scruff who'd been driven away by those two men just a few days ago.

The trace memory of that incident was still strong in her mind. Whoever those men had been, they carried some powerful psychic baggage. The quiet one was a mysterious void, protected and aloof, but the other, the one who had tried to strangle Payne, he was an open door. No defences whatever, a reeking, open sewer. He didn't like seeing inside himself. That's all Payne had done. Turned the camera of his mind inwards. So simple, and yet the effect had been so startling.

Since that day she'd not seen Payne at all. Now he was back, clean-shaven, hair cut and neatly combed, wearing a smart suit and tie. Sonia had seen this change before. She knew why. He had an assignment.

He didn't want the distraction of other people's vibrations; he needed to focus his mind. It wasn't a good omen as far as she was concerned.

She followed him from one room to the next, watched him pull a suitcase from a cupboard and begin to pack.

'You're leaving?' she asked.

'I'm working,' he replied.

'Can I help?'

'No.'

'I'm hurting, Harry.'

He turned towards her, cupping her face in his hands.

'I've told you before,' he said. 'The mind is a house with a thousand locked doors. To open those doors all you need is the key. In your case, the key is pain.' His mouth twitched into a fleeting grin at the unintended pun. 'You're meant to hurt,' he told her.

'But not like this!' Her voice took on a petulant tone. 'You promised to help me,' she pouted.

He rounded on her, his eyes glowing redly.

'Do you want it so badly?' he asked.

Sonia nodded eagerly. 'Yes, oh yes,' she replied. 'I'll die if I don't, Harry, I'll just die!'

'You may do that anyway,' he warned her. 'Once opened the door can rarely be closed.'

'I don't want it closed, I want to free my mind. I want to be like you.'

He smiled a predatory smile. 'Maybe,' he whispered. 'Maybe you do. Follow me,' he ordered.

They left the flat. He walked at a brisk pace, not speaking, just staring straight ahead. Sonia hurried to keep up. There was excitement in the air, she could sense it. For nearly half an hour they walked. Past the residential district, through the market-place, deserted at this time of night, down through the crumbling warehouse district to the riverside. They followed the river for ten minutes, passing through the dilapidated Victorian arches into what everyone called No-Man's-Land.

Once it was a thriving community; now it was derelict, mostly flattened, the occasional rotting street of dead houses standing as mute testimony to what had been.

Carpeted with weeds, rusting cars with no wheels, rubbish and cast-offs, it was home to vermin, both four-legged and two-legged.

In the distance flickering lights danced against the city skyline, flames from a makeshift bonfire. Shadows moved around the flames, the sound of an occasional voice drifting towards them with the smell of woodsmoke. Payne stopped walking and stood very still. Sonia caught up with him and stood by his side, panting slightly.

'What do you see?' he asked her.

Sonia took in her surroundings. 'Winos,' she said. 'Rubbish, demolished houses . . .' She trailed off.

'Close your eyes,' he ordered.

She did as she was told.

'Now what do you see?' he asked her again.

Sonia took a deep breath and opened her mind. The vibrations were old, stale, mean. She sensed the urgency of a fox, scavenging for food, the bitter-sweet cruelty of a big old rat, lying in wait for prey. There was more, but it was beyond her grasp, mocking her, refusing to reveal itself, as coy as a virgin bride on her wedding night.

'I see,' she began, 'I see . . .'

'Nothing.' Payne finished the sentence for her. 'Because you are blind. The door to sight is closed to you. Let's see if we can turn the key, shall we?'

Payne came and stood behind her and placed his hands against the sides of her face. He pressed gently. Sonia stiffened and gasped for breath. The sensation was like plunging into ice-cold water. Her whole body tingled as though charged with static electricity. A sharp bolt of pain stabbed into her head. She screamed. At least, she thought she screamed. Someone standing next to her would have heard the faintest of whimpers. The bones of her skull began to vibrate, a terrible pressure building inside her head. A thin trickle of blood ran from one nostril, moving with maddening slowness past the side of her mouth. Her entire body became ultra-sensitive, the rub of her clothes felt as though they were scouring her skin raw, the faint night breeze became an icy blast, the warmth of Payne's hands upon her face seemed hot enough to sear the flesh from her bones.

And then, something inside her exploded. Sonia gasped. So great was the release of pressure, her whole body felt empty, a limp sack of flesh and disjointed bones. Until something rushed in to fill the void.

Impressions, visions, hallucinations, call them what you will. They rushed in upon her and filled her up, consuming her. She still saw the fire, but now it was a raging inferno; the shadows that shuffled in its glow were large, monstrous, prehistoric shapes, charging and clashing together, bellowing their rage in impotent fury. She felt their pain and their hopelessness, and then something blotted them out. She saw houses, shops, people, saw this desolate spot as it was in its prime, teeming with life and people and hope.

Then it changed. Her skin crawled as disease ravaged the neighbourhood, the searing, pointless destruction caused by the war. She saw flesh rot on bones and living corpses crushing the hopes and dreams of hundreds of people. Just as she had felt their hopes and dreams, so too did she feel their utter black despair. She cried. Great sobbing gulps as she fell to her knees, covering her face with her hands, her entire body heaving with the overwhelming power of her visions.

Payne released her. He watched her until the convulsions stopped. With an exhausted moan Sonia sat back on her haunches, her face streaked with tears and blood. Payne stood in front of her, looking down into her eyes.

'What do you see?' he asked quietly.

It began as a moan, deep inside her, rising up to emerge as laughter: wild, abandoned, hysterical laughter.

'Everything,' she shouted. 'I see everything!'

'And what do you want to see?' he asked.

'More!' she screamed. 'I want to see more, more, more!'

Slowly, like a balloon deflating, she fell forward, resting her head on the hard ground. She turned on her side and curled up into a ball. She was asleep.

Payne bent forward and brushed her hair from her eyes. A soft, satisfied smile graced her lips.

'Maybe you can help me after all,' he mused.

Chapter 26

Warlord was not a happy man.

Christina Laker shifted uncomfortably as he slammed the newspaper onto the desk in front of her.

'Quickly and quietly!' he roared. 'Were those not my instructions as to how this operation should be run?'

The banner headline stared up at her accusingly.

'CLUB OWNER SLAIN', it read.

Christina shuddered. 'With all due respect, sir,' she began, 'I still feel we can contain the damage . . .'

'Respect be damned!' Warlord cut her off. 'This whole affair is a fiasco! I want to know what you're doing about it?'

Christina cleared her throat. She'd rarely seen Warlord this angry. Does he feel responsible? she asked herself. After all, Charlatan was, almost literally, his baby!

'Payne is *in situ* at the moment,' she said. 'The local police have been instructed to provide him with every co-operation. It's just a matter of time.'

'We don't have time.' Warlord's voice was calm now. Beneath the red flush of anger he looked grey and old. Funny, Christina thought, I'd never considered him mortal enough to age like the rest of us.

'Does Payne have any back-up?' Warlord asked.

'None requested, sir. If he needs any, he usually makes his own arrangements.'

'But you can contact him?'

'I have a location and he has a personal communicator with a secure line.'

Warlord grunted. 'At least that part of the operation is by the book.' He picked up the offending newspaper and dumped it in the bin. As he resumed his seat his manner was brisk and businesslike once more.

'Get down there,' he ordered. 'I want you to hold Payne's hand on this one.'

'Sir?'

'I can't explain why, but it's imperative that once Payne has made a positive identification of the subject, you are to take control of the retrieval exercise.'

'If you feel that's best, sir.'

'I do. And don't send him back to Denby either. I've made arrangements with our cousins across the pond to baby-sit for a while. Somewhere pleasant in Washington State, I believe. Our people to supervise, of course. Just a holding operation until the dust settles. Payne will have no further involvement in this case once this operation is over, not even on Charlatan's return. Is that clear?'

'May I ask why, sir? Payne has been remarkably effective with Charlatan.'

'I'm well aware of that, Tina, but I have my reasons. Just do as I say.'

There was a strange look in Warlord's eyes that Christina had never seen before. A look almost of pleading.

'Very well, sir,' she said. 'I'll be *in situ* by lunchtime.'

Chapter 27

She was sitting cross-legged on the hotel bedroom floor.

Her eyes were closed, her breathing shallow, her naked body damp with a cold, clammy sweat. Payne sat in an armchair and watched her. Sonia really was proving to be a most remarkable student. He had had several over the years. Some burnt out early, some never reached their true potential, most proved disappointing in some way or another. In Sonia, it seemed, he had found someone almost as hungry as he was himself.

Of course, Charlatan had been an exceptional student as well, but his power was different: physical as opposed to cerebral. Charlatan's mind had been a labyrinth of dead ends and inconsequentials. Payne had enjoyed being his puppet master, keeping him in line, but programming can only do so much. Charlatan never had the taste for it like Sonia, and he finally rebelled, resisted all attempts to communicate, until finally Payne had to go in. Attack his mind as if it were an armed fortress.

Poor Charlie. You thought you were so clever, hiding away like that. I always knew where to find you, Charlie. I just wanted you to stay hidden, that's all. Walled in, buried, too frightened to come out, locked up in your own little world in a very small corner of your mind. That way I could do what I wanted with the rest. Once you were buried so deep that you'd never find your way out again, I could start to rebuild. Layer upon layer of alternative personality, someone entirely new, someone hungry, someone like me. Oh, it's pure ego, I know, but what better role model could you have? I wanted you to live it all, Charlie, right from the first primal thrill. We were so close to achieving that, Charlie, that's why you responded the way you did; it was me coming out in you. Your very own Mr Hyde.

Chess.

Payne stood up. It was time to check in at the station. Find out if the plodders had unearthed anything of interest.

Payne touched Sonia on the shoulder. She sucked in a deep breath, her whole body rippling. So sensitive, he mused, so very sensitive.

'Find him for me,' he whispered.

Sonia made a low, moaning sound. The air in the room seemed to condense, the light fading, just for a second, as though it were twilight, drawing towards her, surrounding her body with a thin, dark line. Then the line broke up, shattering like glass, each shard growing, taking shape.

Birds. Dark, ethereal birds that swooped and fluttered and then took flight, phantoms of thought that passed through bricks and mortar with consummate ease.

Payne smiled, pleased with his decision. It should save him quite a bit of time and energy.

He left her sitting there, closing the door softly behind him, placing the 'Do Not Disturb' notice on the handle as he left.

Charlie was dreaming.

It was a nice dream. He was wearing his Presley face and he was on stage with Molly and Billy, and the audience loved him! He could do no wrong. They were cheering and clapping, and Molly looked so happy and proud of him, he thought he would burst! He took his bow and ran off stage into the darkness of the wings. He looked back, expecting Molly and Billy to be right behind him, but they were still on stage, and the stage was suddenly so far away, at the end of a long black tunnel.

'Charlie.'

Someone was calling his name. The voice sounded familiar, but he couldn't quite place it. He turned away from the stage, towards the sound of the voice.

Nothing but blackness surrounded him, but there, in the distance, something glowed. Just a pin-prick of light, but it drew him like a moth to a flame. He began to walk towards it.

Gradually the shape in the distance grew bigger. The light changed from a pin-prick to a shimmer, and it took on shape and substance. It was a mirror! A full-length mirror reflecting the blackness all around it.

Something moved in that mirror. His own reflection, maybe? As he drew nearer he realised it wasn't his own reflection he was looking at, it didn't move when he did, but there was something there, something inside the mirror itself!

Finally, he was standing right in front of it, but it was so dark he couldn't see clearly; the shape was indistinct and the mirror radiated coldness, like standing in front of an open freezer door.

And then a slow, dim light appeared within the mirror, growing in intensity until Charlie could make out the figure being reflected back at him.

The Bad Man!

Charlie couldn't move a muscle; he was rooted to the spot.

The Bad Man smiled at him.

'Hello, Charlie,' he said. 'I've come for you, just like I said I would.'

'Nooooooo!' Charlie howled. 'I won't let you take me, I won't!'

The Bad Man laughed.

'You have no choice, Charlie,' he said. 'You have no choice.'

And he stepped forward. Out of the mirror, glass shattering in all directions, cutting Charlie's nice new face to ribbons.

'Too bad about your face, Charlie,' he said. 'Perhaps you'd like to try mine?'

The Bad Man reached up and dug his fingers into his own flesh, right beneath the jawbone. Shoved them right in and pulled. His skin gave way with a wet, ripping sound and he pulled his face right off and held it out to Charlie.

Beneath the Bad Man's face there was another one. Streaked in blood, but instantly recognisable.

It was Charlie's face. His real face, staring back at him.

'You see, Charlie?' the Bad Man said. 'You can't escape me, because I am you!'

And he began to laugh, and laugh, and laugh . . .

Charlie woke up screaming. Drenched in sweat, his body convulsing. It was light in the room. They had been working until the early hours and had slept till nearly noon, but Charlie still felt the blackness clinging to him, suffocating him.

Molly reached out to hold him, but he jerked away from her.

'Charlie?' Sleep and concern made her voice husky and muted. 'What's wrong, Charlie? It's just a dream, that's all, just a dream.'

No, it wasn't just a dream. Charlie knew that, but had no way to explain it. And then he saw the bird. Dark, indistinct, hiding high up in the corner of the room. It looked straight at him, or he thought it did, because it had no eyes. Then it swooped low over his head and flew away, straight through the closed window.

Charlie collapsed into Molly's arms.

'The Bad Man,' he sobbed. 'The Bad Man is here!'

Miles away in a hotel bedroom, a naked girl collapsed onto the floor like a puppet with its strings cut. She lay there for several minutes while dozens of fluttering black shadows gathered in the room. They settled on her motionless body, covering her completely. Slowly they melted, like ice in the sun, absorbed into her skin. She stirred, roused herself onto all fours, panting heavily, her hair curtaining her eyes. She raised her head, and her lips pulled back in a savage grin.

'I've found him,' she said. 'I've found him!'

It was Mike's persistent banging on the door that roused them the next morning. Billy stumbled his way to let him in. Mike shoved a cardboard box into his arms.

'Come on, come on,' he said. 'Can't waste time sleeping. We've got to get to the bunker and start putting some new songs together.'

'New songs?' said Billy, bewildered. 'We don't do new songs. Do we?'

'We do now,' Mike replied cheerfully. 'And pack a bag,' he instructed. 'We'll be living at the bunker for the next few days.'

Molly stuck her head out from beneath the blankets.

'What are you talking about?' she asked.

Mike ripped open the cardboard box that Billy still held in his arms, reached inside and pulled out a flyer.

'This is what I'm talking about,' he said, holding it up for them all to see. 'We have just six days to make rock history.'

Molly looked at the flyer.

'Oh, my God,' she said. 'Oh, my God!'

Chapter 28

*'Lenny Pepper
Hot Stuff!'*

That's how the jingle went. And truer words were never spoken in Lenny's opinion. The fifteen-year-old nymphet who shared his bed last night may have disagreed, but she knew better than to say so.

What the hell was her name, anyway? Tracey? Trixie? Tanya? Who cares? By tomorrow she'll be history.

Lenny left her sleeping and padded into the bathroom to shower. His hair was waiting for him by the washbasin.

'Morning, Barnet,' he said, and patted it affectionately.

Lenny was one of those unfortunate people who didn't have a single hair on their entire body. There was a name for it, but Lenny couldn't remember what it was. It freaked some people out when they first saw him in all his hairless glory, but Lenny wasn't bothered by it. The wig was just for promotional purposes. Hey, showbiz is all about image, right?

His first producer had once said to him, 'Lenny, you're a radio DJ. The listeners haven't a clue if you're bald, pin-striped or hairy as a were-wolf!'

His first producer had been a jerk. There were signed photos to think about, personal appearances and, once, he had been first reserve for 'Celebrity Squares' on TV! Besides, Lenny liked his wig. He thought it made him look like a fatter, whiter Jimi Hendrix. Which was fine with Lenny, because for three years now he had been the heavy-metal guru of Avalon Radio, the fastest growing commercial station in the country. So they said.

The doorbell rang just as Lenny was towelling himself dry. It was bound to be Marjorie; the woman was never late. His playmate of the previous evening was still sleeping soundly, so Lenny grabbed a robe and shut the bedroom door behind him.

'Hi, Marj!' he greeted her jovially. 'Want some breakfast?'

'It's Marjorie, and I ate breakfast at breakfast time. It's now eleven-thirty.'

Marjorie bustled in. She was thin, bespectacled, late twenties and harassed as hell. She was loaded down with tapes, records and promotional material. She was Lenny's Personal Assistant (he shared her with three other Jocks, but he knew she liked him best), and just about ran his life for him.

Lenny busied himself making some freshly squeezed orange juice, while Marjorie unloaded her packages and fired instructions at him, machine-gun fashion.

'We need to sort out the running order for tonight's show. You have a million new releases to review. They're all crap; I've heard them. Can you cover the Godzilla Brothers' gig tomorrow night? Damien's pulled out because of his veins. Your tailor rang to say your shirts are ready. We need a new batch of autographed photos, and please, nothing disgusting this time.'

Lenny watched her bustling about like a miniature whirlwind. It was better than a Roadrunner cartoon!

'What's that?' he said, pointing to a package Marjorie had deposited on the table.

'Dunno,' she replied. 'It arrived for you at the station just before I left, so I brought it along.'

Lenny put down his orange juice and picked the parcel up. It was quite heavy. Lenny liked opening parcels. It reminded him of Christmas.

The bedroom door opened and Tracey/Trixie/Tanya walked in, quite naked, rubbing sleep from her eyes.

'Got any Coco Pops?' she asked.

Lenny jerked his thumb towards the kitchen.

'In there,' he said.

'Thanks,' the girl replied, and wandered lethargically away.

Marjorie was peering at him accusingly over her spectacles.

'She's my niece,' Lenny explained, lamely.

'And I'm your Aunt Fanny!' Marjorie responded.

'Then let's keep it in the family, shall we, "Aunty"?' Lenny suggested.

'Just don't come running to me when you're all over the Sunday papers, Len, that's all.'

'I won't. And the name's Lenny, Marj.'

'Touché. Where do you want to start?'

'With this.' Lenny had finished unwrapping his parcel. It contained a cassette and a pile of flyers.

'That sly old fox!' Lenny commented.

'Who?'

'Sidney Brass.'

'Hellfire Club? That Sidney Brass?'

'That's him. Seems he has a new discovery making their début on Saturday.'

'So?'

'So, I think we ought to know about it, don't you, Marjorie?'

'Why? The place is a dump. A toilet for bikers and Brass is a moron whose knuckles scrape the ground when he walks.'

Lenny sighed. 'The Hellfire Club is one of the premier venues for alternative rock culture,' he corrected her. 'And Mr Brass is an entrepreneur of some standing in the music fraternity. Besides, bikers make up a large part of my listening figures, Marjorie!'

'You have a point there,' she agreed.

'Sidney and I are usually on good terms,' Lenny mused. 'But he's kept this one under wraps. Luckily the little darlings have shown some initiative and sent me a demo themselves.' He passed the flyers to Marjorie.

'Yuck!' she said.

The kitchen door opened and Tracey/Trixie/Tanya emerged, eating cereal from a bowl.

'You were out of Coco Pops,' she informed him. 'So I had Corn Flakes instead.' She ate her way into the bedroom and kicked the door shut behind her.

Marjorie raised an eyebrow at Lenny, which was more than he could do, but didn't say a word.

'Let's play the tape,' Lenny suggested.

Ten minutes later Lenny was on the phone to Sidney Brass to discuss the possibility of broadcasting Saturday's show live from the Hellfire Club.

Chapter 29

Do this, do that, do the other! If he sits down I'll bloody well sing to him!

Chief Superintendent Piggott was not in a good mood. The 'spook' had arrived and wanted to see everything that had been compiled so far. And could he speak to the officer in charge of the case?

No, he sodding well couldn't, because Detective Inspector Bannerman had gone walkabout in the middle of a murder investigation, chasing ghosts from twenty-odd years ago!

It irked Piggott to admit that Bannerman's theory held at least some water. He just wished the man would be a bit more orthodox in his methods.

'Rafferty!' Piggott shouted across the canteen.

Rafferty jumped and nearly choked on a mouthful of spotted dick.

'Yes, sir?' he mumbled around a mouthful of custard.

'Where's Bannerman?' Piggott asked.

'Pursuing inquiries, sir.'

'I know that, Rafferty. I mean where is he precisely, and are we likely to be graced by his presence some time in the near future?'

'He phoned in this morning, sir. Didn't actually say where he was, but not to expect him back today. Said to carry on with the usual routine.'

'The usual routine!' Piggott spluttered. 'This is a murder hunt, not a bloody circus!'

'Yes, sir,' said Rafferty meekly.

'Right,' Piggott continued. 'As he's not here, you'll have to do it.'

'Do what, sir?'

'Play nursemaid to that snooper from London. He wants everything we've turned up so far on his desk in an hour.'

'Yes, sir,' Rafferty replied.

'Oh, and one more thing.' There was an evil gleam in Piggott's eye. 'He also wants to see the corpse. Take him down to the morgue as soon as you've had your lunch, will you?'

Piggott turned on his heel and marched out.

Suddenly Rafferty had lost his appetite.

'Come on, Sid. I've heard the tape; this guy's brilliant!'

It was Lenny Pepper's third call to Sidney Brass in two hours.

'I tell you,' Brass growled, 'I don't know what you're talking about!'

'Stop kidding around, Sid,' Lenny wheedled. 'The posters are all over town.'

'I know,' Brass growled. 'Some bastard's even plastered them all over the front of the club!'

'And you really have no idea what's going on?'

'For the last time, no!'

'I'll call you back, Sid. Ciao.'

Lenny sat for a while, thinking. If this is a hoax, someone's gone to a lot of trouble if they don't intend to show up. Maybe Sid doesn't know anything about it, not yet anyway, but Saturday is still three days away.

'Okay,' he told Marjorie. 'We go with it. Reschedule tonight's show with this as the main feature. Find out everything you can in the meantime. See if we can get some guests in. I have a gut feeling this is going to be big!'

'Are you sure it's not just indigestion?' she asked him.

The Morgue Attendant was a vulture.

A great, hump-backed bird pecking at the remains of the dead. The spirits of the newly departed clustered around him, pleading to be let go, to be returned to life, or simply bemoaning their fate. He struck out at them with his cruel beak and they withdrew, cringing and cowed.

'You're mine now,' he screeched, 'and you're not going anywhere until I say so!'

The image was rather a cliché, Payne had to admit, but he had difficulty blocking it out. A blue pill would take care of that, but he resisted.

The vulture opened a shiny steel cabinet and wheeled out its current occupant. He unzipped the body bag with his beak so that Payne could see properly.

Jarvis's lingering spirit crouched like a large, black spider on his chest. It was a mean spirit, spiteful and weak. Payne smiled at it and it scuttled away.

Payne was more interested in the other vibrations. The images of Rick Jarvis's last few minutes of life lingered over his corpse like a cloud of rancid perfume. Payne breathed them in hungrily, and the scene unfolded before his mind's eye.

It was late, nearly two in the morning. Video Dome was about to close. Jarvis wasn't expecting callers, but Stevey was always welcome. Payne sensed the trauma that came next, building like a volcano. First, the nagging impression that something wasn't quite right. Then the fire-alarm clamour that signalled danger. Then pain, helplessness, panic and despair. Finally, oh yes, finally, but not before the agony and the destruction of both mind and body, came the sweet release of death.

Charlatan's aura was unmistakable. You did well, Charlie, but you still have a bit to learn. The video was a nice touch, but you didn't know your subject well enough, even the plods saw through that one! And the message on the wall was a definite mistake; could get us all in a lot of trouble with that, Charlie.

'Have you seen enough, sir?' the vulture asked.

'Oh, yes,' Payne replied quietly. 'It's been most enlightening.'

'Darth Presley? Who's he?'

'The Dark Spirit of Rock, just like it says.' Cathy handed Susan one of the flyers that had been appearing all over town. It was lunchtime and they were sitting against the chain-link fence that bordered the playing fields. The poster was blue with black letters.

I AM THE RESURRECTION AND THE ROCK AND ROLL!

The Dark Spirit of Rock will be conjured up, live on stage, at the Hellfire Club this Saturday night.

Be there to witness the first mortal incarnation of DARTH PRESLEY, direct from the bowels of Heavy Metal Hell!

Witches and Warlocks half price!

'It's tacky,' Susan commented.

'Should be a blast!' Cathy grinned.

'Are you going?'

'Sure. Zeke's taking me.'

Susan looked sceptical.

'Well, I've not actually seen him since this came out,' Cathy admitted, 'but I'm sure he's going. He's really into heavy metal and black magic, and all sorts of stuff like that. He'll take me, I'm sure.'

'I hope you know what you're doing.' Susan handed back the flyer.

'I do,' Cathy replied. 'I absolutely do!'

Payne wasn't answering his calls.

Blast the man! Christina dumped her bags in her room. Without bothering to unpack, she set off on the five-minute walk that would take her to the hotel where Payne was staying. If he's not here I'll have to try the station, she thought. She was loath to do that. It was better if she didn't have to tip her hand just yet to the local police. Time enough for that when Charlatan was positively identified.

Christina knew which room she wanted. There was a 'Do Not Disturb' sign on the door. She ignored it and knocked loudly.

The door opened, but it wasn't Payne.

Sonia was naked, but didn't seem to care. Her eyes were glazed, but came into focus as she recognised the woman standing on the threshold.

'You must be Christina,' she said. 'Harry's told me about you.'

Christina raised a quizzical eyebrow. 'Has he?' she said.

'Oh, don't worry,' Sonia replied. 'None of the secret stuff. Just enough to make it interesting.'

'Can I come in?' Christina asked, 'or do you intend to give everyone a cheap thrill?'

Sonia shrugged, as though it was a matter of complete indifference to her, but stepped back to let Christina enter.

Christina closed the door behind her. Sonia curled up on the bed and watched her through half-closed eyes.

She's his type, Christina thought. Barely more than a child, really. Something wild about her, though; half tame, half jungle beast. I hope you know what you're doing, Harry.

'Where is he?' Christina asked.

'Out,' Sonia replied, tartly.

'I can see that. When will he be back?'

Sonia shrugged. 'Later, I suppose. He didn't say.'

'Damn! I need to talk to him urgently. If he should get in touch, can you tell him I called?'

'Sure.'

Christina turned to go.

'I know where he is,' said Sonia softly.

Christina turned back.

'Who?' she asked.

Sonia laughed. 'Charlatan, of course,' she said. 'That is who you're looking for, isn't it?'

'So tell me, Sid, is there really going to be a Black Mass at the Hellfire Club on Saturday night?'

They were live on air and Lenny Pepper was enjoying himself watching Brass squirm.

'Of course not!' Brass snapped. 'I know nothing about all this.'

'But you do play "heavy metal" music, do you not?' The Reverend Malcolm Preedy had a thin, nasal voice that was designed to irritate. He was Lenny's pet vicar who was wheeled out any time Lenny wanted to stir up an argument.

'Yes,' Brass conceded. 'We're a heavy metal club, so what?'

'I think it is well established,' said Preedy smugly, 'that the forces of darkness use that particular medium to spread the satanic message to young and impressionable minds.'

Brass looked as if he wanted nothing more than to tie a reef knot in the Reverend Preedy's scrawny neck.

'And whether you know anything about it or not, Sid,' Lenny interrupted, 'it appears that your establishment has been chosen by this particular "dark force" as the venue for his first public appearance in this universe. Let me read you a message that was delivered to this station this afternoon.'

Brass glowered at him. He hadn't been told about any message!

Lenny produced a piece of paper and began to read.

'Know you, that the time has come for the Dark Spirit of Rock to walk among you. He has sent his voice from the other side to foretell his coming. He shall not be denied. In a ceremony older than time he will walk from the Hellfire to imbue the rotting corpse of Rock with his Dark Majesty's most glorious essence. Be there if you dare to witness the diabolical incarnation of the one and only Darth Presley!'

Lenny paused for breath.

'Phew!' he continued. 'Heavy stuff! And a direct reference to the Hellfire Club, wouldn't you say, Sid?'

'I . . . uh . . . I . . .' Brass spluttered.

'How about you, Reverend?' Lenny smarmed.

'It's perfectly obvious,' said Preedy sniffily, 'that some malignant force has chosen to use Mr Brass's establishment as the focal point for some demonic exercise. Drawn, no doubt, by its already dubious emanations. Whether Mr Brass gives his permission or not is quite irrelevant.'

'So, what would you advise?'

'A thorough exorcism seems the only answer!' Preedy replied with a self-satisfied smile.

'Well,' Lenny continued, 'perhaps you could say a quick prayer for us now, Father, because here is the man himself, Darth Presley, exclusive to Avalon Radio and "Voices From The Other Side"!'

There was a monster lurking under Colin's bed.

He knew that because his parents had always told him so.

'If you're a bad boy,' they would say, 'God won't love you any more and he'll feed you to the monster under your bed.'

Colin tried so hard to be good, but the monster was still there. He could hear it at night, slithering and sucking and scraping with its claws, and sometimes it would talk to him, calling his name, trying to get him to do bad things. And now it had a face, with long, greasy hair and HATE tattooed across its forehead. Oh, that was the face of the monster all right, and it had captured Cathy! Someone should have told her about the monster. Colin had tried, but she wouldn't listen, and now it had her in its clutches. But Colin could still save her, oh yes, he could. All he had to do was kill the monster and its hold over Cathy would be broken.

But first he had to find the monster.

Colin listened to his new transistor radio and he smiled.

'I know where you'll be on Saturday night, monster,' he crooned. 'I know where you'll be, and I'll be waiting.'

Sonia sat curled up at Payne's feet. He reached out to stroke her hair and she responded by rubbing her face against his hand, much as a pet cat may do.

At least she's wearing something now! Christina thought.

Payne smiled. There was a barbed wire fence between the two women and it amused him greatly. They stood in Billy's living room and surveyed the debris of a rock-'n'-roll existence.

'He was here,' Payne confirmed.

'And now?' Christina snapped. Today had been a bad day for her, full of frustrations. Payne had remained at the station until late afternoon, going over the latest developments in the police investigation. Sonia had petulantly refused to give out any more information, and had finally curled up and gone to sleep. Christina had stormed out of the room and returned some hours later. This time Payne was in residence. It had taken them just over thirty minutes to reach Billy's flat, and less than thirty seconds to pick the lock.

Payne frowned, and paused before answering her question.

'He's . . .' he hesitated, '. . . gone to ground,' he finished. 'Some kind of interference, electrical possibly, or a natural shield of some kind.'

'So what do we do now?' Christina asked.

Payne bent down and picked up a piece of paper that had become wedged beneath a chair. A slow smile spread across his face.

'What are you doing Saturday night?' he asked.

Christina frowned, and he handed her the flyer advertising Darth Presley's début.

'Don't you see?' Payne laughed. 'It's brilliant! The perfect cover for someone like Charlatan.'

'You mean he's actually part of this "Darth Presley" set-up?'

Payne shrugged. 'Why not?' He gestured at the musical detritus that surrounded them. 'All the evidence points to it, wouldn't you say?'

'Okay,' she conceded. 'If you're right, then you should be able to make a positive identification on the spot.'

'Correct.'

'And you're clear about the new instructions?'

Payne nodded. 'We find him, you reel him in. What I don't understand is why?'

'Orders,' Christina snapped.

'And you always obey orders, don't you, Christina?'

Payne's face twisted into a sly smile. There was a molten core deep in the heart of Christina Laker. A secret that haunted her still. She'd killed her lover. Shot him through the head as he slept. He was a traitor, it's true, but it still tore at her soul. She had been following orders when she pulled the trigger. Warlord's orders. It was her rite of passage. From that day on he knew he had her, body and soul. She was still following his orders, but the memory remained at the back of her mind. Payne had seen it there many times, skulking, haunting.

Christina looked at him, saw that familiar smile. It was a smile that said, 'I know a secret. And it's yours!' She flushed, but didn't react to the bait.

'Just do your job, Harry,' she told him. 'Just do your job.'

Chapter 30

She was the twelfth name on his list.

He didn't hold out much hope. Four days of raking up painful memories had produced no worthwhile results. It was too long ago. Nobody remembered, nobody wanted to remember.

How many more straws will you clutch at before you finally drown? he asked himself.

Just one more, he promised.

Sandy Caldwell. Sandy Maxwell now. Twenty-four years ago a young PC Bannerman had taken her statement. Maybe it will turn out to be a lucky omen.

Sandy Maxwell lived at 27 Kitchener Road. It was a run-down council house with a scrubby front garden and a satellite dish that had no doubt fallen off a passing satellite.

Two youths aged between Borstal and Strangeways were kicking a deflated football about the front garden and swigging lager from cans at the same time.

Bannerman pushed open a gate that screeched like the three witches from Macbeth. The two youths eyed him malevolently. As he walked forward, the taller of the two barred his way.

'Wot you want?' the youth asked.

'Yeah, wot you want, eh?' the smaller version repeated.

'Peace and understanding between the nations of the world,' Bannerman replied, dead-pan.

They blinked, one after the other. Bannerman could almost smell the circuits of their brains burning out as they tried to work out what he'd just said.

'You a poofta?' the tall one asked eventually.

'Yeah, you a poofta, or what?' said Little Sir Echo.

'Nice parrot you have there,' Bannerman remarked. 'Can he do any other tricks?'

'You're lookin' for a good kickin'.' Lofty stated.

'Yeah . . .' Shorthouse began, but Bannerman raised a hand to stop him.

'Don't say it,' he advised. 'I couldn't stand it if you said something different!'

I shouldn't be doing this, he told himself. It's a battle of wits and my opponents are unarmed!

'Jason! Wayne!' The harridan lilt came from the direction of the front door. Both youths turned in unison.

I wonder which is Jason and which is Wayne? Bannerman pondered. He glanced towards the door.

The years had not been kind to Sandy Caldwell. He knew from her record that she had a string of arrests, mainly shoplifting and prostitution, but even so she was a far cry from the pretty young thing whose statement he had taken all those years ago.

'Mrs Maxwell?' Bannerman called.

'Who wants to know?'

'Detective Inspector Bannerman.'

Jason and Wayne made audible hissing noises. They looked like they would have made the sign of the cross if it would have done any good.

'Can I have a few words?' Bannerman asked.

'If you like,' she replied cautiously. 'But it'll have to be quick; I'm expecting company in half an hour.'

'The Archbishop of Canterbury, no doubt,' Bannerman muttered under his breath, as he walked steadfastly into the lion's den.

Sandy Maxwell was wearing black high heels and fishnet stockings. Anything else she may, or may not, have been wearing was hidden by a pink housecoat. For that Bannerman was eternally grateful. Her hair was held back by a black band and her lipstick had bled onto her teeth. She invited him into what she called the 'lounge', and he took a seat in a dubious-looking armchair.

'Don't mind those two,' she said, indicating Bannerman's recent debating society members. 'They're just kids. What can you do with them, eh?'

Several possibilities came to mind but, for once, Bannerman was tactful enough to keep quiet.

'Want a cuppa?' she asked.

Bannerman took in the general state of his surroundings, applied that knowledge in good detective fashion to assess the probable state of the kitchen, and said:

'No, thank you, Mrs Maxwell.'

'Call me Sandy,' she said. 'No one's called me "Mrs Maxwell" since me old man left me, and that was nearly six years ago!'

She sat down on the sofa and crossed her legs, straightening the hem of her housecoat demurely.

'What is it you want?' she asked.

'You probably don't remember me,' Bannerman began. 'It was a long time ago when we last met. Twenty-four years ago, to be precise.'

Sandy peered at him. 'Blimey!' she said. 'I thought I recognised you from somewhere. Haven't you put on weight!'

Bannerman shifted uncomfortably. 'A lot can happen in twenty-four years,' he said darkly.

'Don't I know it!' Sandy agreed. 'You're not still after him, are you?'

'Who?'

'That Chess bloke. The one who killed Debbie.'

'We think there may be a connection with a recent homicide, yes.'

'Bloody hell!'

'You may have read about it in the papers.'

'Don't read the papers much. Haven't got the time.'

'I hear Richard Branson has the same problem.'

Sandy stared at him blankly, the barb falling well short of its mark.

'So, what do you want with me, eh?' she asked. 'I told you all I knew at the time. I'm not likely to remember anything now, am I?'

'Do you remember Marcus Knight?'

As near as could be ascertained beneath the make-up, the colour drained from Sandy's face.

'Yes, I remember Marcus,' she said slowly.

'Can you tell me something about him?'

'He was a friend of Debbie's. You don't think he killed her, do you?'

'We're just tying up some loose ends, that's all.'

'After all this time!'

'The wheels of justice grind exceedingly slow,' Bannerman intoned ponderously. 'Now, if you could cast your mind back. Anything at all may be of help.'

Sandy fished in the pocket of her housecoat, produced a packet of cigarettes and a lighter, took a cigarette from the pack, lit it and inhaled deeply.

'I was nineteen,' she said. 'You wouldn't believe it now, but I was good looking then. Not in Debbie's class, though. She was something special. She'd have made it as a model if she hadn't . . .' She paused. Unpleasant memories, long since pushed to the back of her mind, crowded forward once more.

'Go on,' Bannerman urged.

'She wasn't like the rest of us,' Sandy continued. 'Debbie, I mean. She had a job, her own flat, everything.' She smiled. 'We used to call her a "weekend hippie". The rest of us, there must have been eight or nine of us at the time, were living in a crummy squat. We called it a "commune", but it was a squat really. Anyway, it was through Debbie that I met Marcus. She just turned up with him one day. You could tell she was crazy about him. It was easy to see why; he was a real smoothy. Could charm the knickers off a nun, could Marcus. But what made him really popular was his "little blue pills". God knows what was in them, but they packed a hell of a kick! I've never had such weird dreams!'

For a second or two, Sandy's face had a far-away look, then she shook her head and sighed deeply. She stubbed out her cigarette in an already overflowing ashtray and lit another.

'Anyway, Marcus fancied me. Well, in those days it was all "free love", so I thought, what the hell? He was a kinky little sod really. Fancied a threesome with me and Debbie. Funny, I didn't think Debs would go for it; she was always a bit strait-laced about that sort of thing.'

'And did she go for it?' Bannerman asked.

'I'll say! Very enthusiastic, as I recall. It became quite a regular thing. I used to call us his "harem". I was never his first choice, though. Debbie was always number one. She used to say they had a special kind of bond between them, whatever that meant. I was just a bit of spare, I suppose, but I didn't bear a grudge. Not at first, anyway. Then she changed for some reason. Got all sorts of airs and graces, treated me like I was the hired help.' Sandy shrugged. 'Well, her career was taking off and I suppose she just outgrew us. She stopped coming round after a while. They both did. I didn't care. Truth is, I knew something about her precious Marcus that even Debbie didn't know.'

'And what was that?' Bannerman asked.

'I knew where he lived.'

Bannerman caught his breath. There had been no mention of an address for Marcus Knight on file!

'Not even Debbie knew that,' Sandy continued. 'He was a bit of a mystery man, was Marcus. He'd just turn up out of the blue, then disappear again when he felt like it. I always thought he had a wife tucked away somewhere, but I never found out for sure. Anyway, I found out where he lived and it gave me a sort of edge over Debbie. I never told her. Just kept it to myself, all smug like. Soppy really, but we were just kids.'

'And how did you find out his address?' Bannerman asked, trying to hide the eagerness in his voice.

'It was a Saturday,' Sandy continued. 'We were supposed to be going to the pictures, all three of us. Then Debbie had to go off on some job or other, so Marcus and me went on our own. Only we never got there. On the way he had some sort of fit. I'd never seen him like this before; he was in a hell of a state. He was moaning and holding his head like it was going to burst. I was dead scared, I can tell you. He wouldn't let me call for an ambulance, though. Said all he needed was to get home and get some more pills.'

'So he gave you his address so that you could take him home?' Bannerman asked.

'Not quite. Even then, you see, he didn't want anyone to know where he lived. He just gave me directions. Miles it was, out Cranburn way, right at the posh end of town. Anyway, we get to this street corner and he says that this is close enough. Wants me to leave him to make his own way there.'

'And did you?'

'Sort of. I was worried, you see. Thought he might collapse in the street. So I followed him. Made sure he got home all right before I left. Didn't see him for a few weeks after that. When he did turn up he was right as rain, never even mentioned it. Things started to go downhill after that. I saw less and less of both of them. Then, the next thing I knew, Debbie was dead and you lot came round asking questions.'

'Why didn't you tell us all this at the time?' Bannerman asked.

'None of your business, was it? Besides, I had other things on my mind.'

'Such as?'

Sandy lit up her third cigarette.

'Oh, what the hell,' she said. 'What difference can it make now? I was pregnant, if you must know.'

Bannerman inclined his head towards the front garden, where Jason and Wayne had recommenced their desultory game of football.

'They don't look old enough,' he said.

'Not them!' Sandy replied. 'They came along much later. No, I had another kid before them. Marcus's kid.'

Bannerman sat up straight.

'You're sure it was his?' he asked.

Sandy laughed. 'Of course I am. I may have slept around, but I wasn't that much of a slag! Well, not then anyway.'

'I didn't mean to suggest . . .' Bannerman flustered.

Sandy waved his protestations away with a plume of smoke.

'S'alright,' she said. 'I know how it must look. It was Marcus's baby all right.'

'And is that why you didn't give us his address? You were protecting him?'

'Not him exactly. Y'see, when I first found out about the baby, I was desperate. I didn't want a baby, for Christ's sake! I had no one to turn to. The weeks went by and he never turned up, so I plucked up courage and went to his house. I knew he'd be mad, but I had to talk to him, get something sorted out.'

'You mean an abortion?'

'He could afford it, and I knew he wouldn't stick by me if I had it, so what other option was there? Anyway, I just turned up one morning on his doorstep.'

'What was his reaction?'

'Never saw him. The chap I spoke to said they were all going away.'

'So, who did you speak to?'

'Said he was Marcus's uncle. Nice bloke. Invited me in, gave me a cup of tea. He could see something was up, so in the end I told him the whole story. He was angry at first, more at Marcus than me, then he calmed down and gave me some money. Fifty quid it was. Said under no circumstances must I have an abortion. He gave me the name of a doctor and said I was to go and see him right away. He'd arrange everything, he said. Money, hospital, the lot. The only condition was that I was never to mention anything about this to Marcus, and I was not to try and find him. Something about spoiling his career.'

'And you did as you were told?'

'Why not? What else was I supposed to do? Anyway, no sooner had I got back than I heard that Debbie had been killed. It never occurred to me that Marcus might have been involved, and I had the baby to consider, not to mention the money . . .'

'So you withheld his address,' Bannerman finished for her.

'That's right.'

'And what happened after that?'

'I just did like I was told. Saw this doctor and he sorted everything. Lovely hospital it was; none of your National Health rubbish.'

'And the baby?'

A small cloud crossed Sandy's face.

'It was deformed,' she said. 'Ugly little bleeder it was. I mean, they all are, but he was disgusting.' She shuddered. 'Very pale skin, no hair, couldn't open his eyes either, poor little bugger, and his mouth was so small I couldn't even get me tit onto it!'

'But what happened to him?' Bannerman persisted.

'I had another visit from Marcus's uncle while I was still in hospital. That's the only other time I saw him. He said he'd been talking to the doctors and the kid was going to need a lot of specialist care. Well, I'd figured that out for myself, hadn't I? He tells me that there's no way I could look after it myself, so maybe I should sign it over into care. He had the papers all drawn up and everything. Well, I wasn't sure at first. I mean, I was the poor little sod's mother after all. Then he says that I've been inconvenienced by all this, and some kind of compensation is due. And he waves a cheque for a thousand pounds under me nose! That was a lot of money in those days.'

'So you signed?'

'I signed. And that was the last I saw of either of them.' She paused. 'You don't really think Marcus killed Debbie, do you?' she asked.

Before Bannerman could answer the doorbell rang.

'That's my "company",' Sandy told him.

'Would you be prepared to come down to the station and make a statement?' he asked. 'Just to get everything that you've just told me down on record?'

She looked at him curiously. The doorbell rang again.

'All right,' she said. 'But I must see to my visitor first.'

Bannerman made to lever himself out of his chair.

'You can stay if you want,' Sandy told him. 'He never takes long. I'll be with you in ten minutes.'

Bannerman sat back down and prepared to wait.

Chapter 31

Sidney 'Knuckles' Brass had the face and the build of the ex-boxer that he was, and the business instincts of a barracuda. Questions were still being asked about the whereabouts of the Hellfire Club's previous owner, but no one dared to voice them in Sidney's presence. Very few things could be said to truly rattle him, but now he was rattled.

He was just twenty-four hours away from what could be the biggest fiasco of his career.

Darth Presley.

Stupid bloody name. Posters had been appearing like confetti all week advertising a début gig at his club that he knew nothing about! 'Knuckles' Brass did not like to be taken for a ride. Pepper knew more about this man than he was telling. Why else would those tapes get sent to him? There had been three so far and that asshole had been playing them on his show non-stop! He was even coming to the gig tomorrow night with a sound crew to broadcast it live! He called it a media event. 'Knuckles' Brass called it something entirely different! Someone was going to pay for this, and pay hard.

It was Friday night and the club was buzzing with talk about Darth Presley. 'Knuckles' sat in his office and brooded. The phone rang and he snatched it up.

'Brass,' he rumbled.

'I can give you Darth Presley,' the voice said. The voice was muffled, indistinct, as though the owner was speaking through a cloth.

'Who the fuck is this?' Brass demanded.

'Hey,' the voice said. 'It's your arse on the line tomorrow night if nobody shows. Do you want him or not?'

Brass ground his teeth in fury. 'Yes,' he said. 'I want him all right.

'Good,' the voice replied. 'Make sure there's someone there to let us in the back door at four o'clock. We'll need a couple of hours to set up and sound check. You won't be sorry.'

The phone went dead.

Brass snarled and slammed the receiver down.

'Damn right I won't be sorry!' he shouted. 'But you, my friend, will wish you had never been born!'

Chapter 32

Bannerman appeared at the station like a thief in the night.

A fat phantom, glimpsed briefly, who vanishes in the morning light.

Sandy Maxwell had come up trumps. Twenty-four years late, but who's counting?

Bannerman issued instructions.

Find out who lived at the Cranburn address in 1969.

Track down the GP who treated Sandy Caldwell.

Check the hospital records. Find out what happened to Sandy's baby.

Bannerman left instructions that a transcript of Sandy's statement be left on Piggott's desk.

The secretary who typed it out, being efficient and keen, remembered that Mr Payne would also need a copy. Such a nice man, Mr Payne. She'd only spoken to him briefly, but it felt as if she had known him for years; so easy to talk to.

She made sure that he got his copy first.

It had been a rough night, so Sandy Maxwell slept late.

Raking up old memories had left her drained. She didn't like to dwell on the past, especially not poor Debbie. And the baby. She had felt no remorse at giving it away; the mothering instinct had not been strong, but she did wonder sometimes what had become of him.

When she finally woke she had a headache. Today was Saturday. No customers today; she always made it a rule to keep the weekends free, so she knew she had time for a nice hot bath.

The doorbell rang when she was up to her neck in bubbles.

'Sod off!' she called, 'whoever you are.'

The doorbell rang again.

'Jason! Wayne!' she called. 'Answer the door!' There was no reply; they'd obviously gone out.

When the doorbell rang a third time, Sandy decided she'd better answer it. Grumbling to herself, she climbed out of the bath, wrapped a towel around her and hurried downstairs, leaving a trail of wet footprints behind her.

She opened the door, and looked back through time.

'Hello, Sandy,' he said. 'My ears are burning. Have you been talking about me?'

When Sandy woke up she was sitting at the bottom of the stairs, naked save for a bath towel that had come loose and had fallen around her feet.

'What am I doing here?' she asked herself.

Something had happened, but she couldn't remember what.

Oh well, she shrugged, if it's important it'll come back to me.

She trudged upstairs to resume her bath, and was surprised to find the water had gone cold.

4.05 Saturday afternoon.

'Knuckles' Brass picked Mike Menagerie up by the throat and shook him until his teeth rattled.

'You miserable little asshole!' Brass snarled.

'P-p-pleease!' Mike stammered. 'I can explain.'

Brass threw him half-way across the room. He landed in a heap.

'You got thirty seconds,' Brass told him.

'It's not the same band,' Mike gasped. 'We found a new lead singer. You've heard the tapes, you know how good he is. We just need a chance. How else could I get one?'

'I don't like being made a fool of.' Brass advanced towards him, fists balled menacingly at his sides.

Mike scurried away on all fours.

'Okay,' he said, 'beat me up, kill me if you want, you've still got a club full of people turning up tonight expecting to see Darth Presley. And the radio, and the papers.'

Brass stopped and considered.

'Let us play,' Mike pleaded. 'Then, if we're no good, it's not your fault. You've said all along you knew nothing about all this. But if we are good . . .' He let that thought sink in for a while.

'Okay,' Brass said. 'You can play. But for your sake you'd better be bleedin' brilliant!'

Outside in the van, Billy drummed impatiently on the dashboard.

'Come on, come on,' he muttered. 'What's taking so long?' Molly sat in the back of the van and gave Charlie's hand an affectionate squeeze. He looked pale and tired. They all did. It had been an exhausting week, especially for Charlie. Rehearsing, doing demo tapes for Lenny Pepper, rewriting Billy's songs so they fitted the new image, sticking posters up all over the place, getting costumes and props together, and a hundred and one other things. And what little sleep they had managed to grab had been disturbed by Charlie's nightmares.

We must be mad to be doing this, thought Molly. Saturation coverage, Mike had called it. Never in a million years did Molly think it would work. But it had! Everyone was talking about it. It had taken every penny they all had to keep the rumour mill turning, but it would all pay off if Brass would now play ball.

'Yes!' Billy shouted triumphantly. 'He's done it!'

Mike had reappeared at the back door to the Hellfire Club and was beckoning them forward. Billy started the engine.

The butterflies in Molly's stomach took flight once more.

It was too late to back out now.

Is that a gun in your pocket, or are you just pleased to see me?

That's what Cathy had said to him the night she had sold herself to those Godless fiends.

She'd meant it as an insult, but what would she say now? Now that there really was a gun in his pocket!

The revolver had belonged to Colin's grandfather, who had brought it back from the war. Colin's father had kept it in very good condition and it was in full working order. Colin hoped he wouldn't get reprimanded for taking it without permission, but it was in a good cause.

Christina looked at Sonia in her lurid tee-shirt and skin-tight jeans and groaned. She felt terribly out of place in her slacks and check shirt, worn loose to hide the bulk of the automatic tucked in at her waist.

They'll think I'm her mother! Christina thought.

'Where's Harry?' she snapped.

Sonia shook her head. Her skin had a waxy cast to it and she was sweating. The rapport she shared with Payne enabled her to tune in on his thoughts, but ever since this afternoon all she was getting was a frantic jumble of conflicting signals. It was making her sick to her stomach.

'I don't know,' she said.

'Are you sick?' Christina asked.

Sonia shook her head. She didn't want to admit the real reason for her discomfort.

'Something I ate,' she lied. 'Are we going or what?'

Christina looked at her watch.

Damn Harry Payne!

'Okay,' she said. 'We'll go on our own. Do you think you can recognise Charlatan, even if he's in another form?'

Sonia nodded.

'All right,' Christina decided. 'Let's do it!'

It was ten minutes until show time and the doors still weren't open. Several hundred people were gathered outside, a veritable sea of denim, leather and chains.

A ragged, impatient cheer went up.

'We want Darth! We want Darth!'

Inside the club Mike Menagerie was feeling sick.

Oh, please God, let this work! he prayed.

Lenny Pepper lounged at the bar, talking to Sidney Brass, waiting to go live on the air.

Talk about being thrown in at the deep end!

Mike gave the set a final once-over.

'All ready?' he asked. Everyone nodded their agreement, too keyed-up to talk. 'Okay,' Mike said. 'Let's do it!'

As soon as the doors opened the crowd let out a roar and surged forward.

Colin pushed his way in amongst them, letting himself be carried by the tide, his right hand jammed firmly in his pocket, holding on tightly to the ancient revolver.

So many people to choose from, but somewhere in the crowd he knew was the face he was looking for. The face with HATE tattooed upon it.

The stage was in darkness.

Strange amorphous shapes huddled in the blackness.

Slowly the lights came up to reveal a signpost; blood-red letters said 'TO HELL', and an arrow pointed downwards.

Across the centre of the stage was a coffin. A woman, dressed in a red basque, torn stockings and fingerless gloves, was slumped across it. Her face was ghostly white, her lips and fingernails jet black. A bass guitar was slung around her neck.

To one side a figure in a ragged trench-coat lounged over some keyboards. His hair was slicked back, his face a greenish grey with blood-red lips. Mirrored shades hid his eyes. He crooked a taloned finger at the audience.

'Come closer,' he rasped, his voice a reptilian hiss. 'I have something to tell you.'

The first piece was an instrumental.

Heavy and fast, the punters stomped along, shouting and clapping.

Colin pushed his way through the crowd. Somewhere up ahead, near the front, he thought he glimpsed a familiar, hateful face. Next to it a small, blonde figure. Cathy?

The music came to an abrupt halt. The crowd cheered. The lights came down and a slow, hypnotic note floated across the footlights.

Suddenly, in a blare of noise and light, the lid of the coffin flew off and an arm appeared, shooting straight up from within the casket. This was no ordinary arm. It had scales. And talons six inches long, and it turned slowly in the spotlight, a venomous snake waiting to strike. Then, with agonising slowness it rose up, dragging the rest of its body behind it. Its back to the audience, the creature from the coffin snarled and growled as the music built to a crescendo. The sound built and built until it was almost too painful to listen to, and then it burst, pounding into a frantic rock beat, and the creature turned, leaping from the coffin and charging the audience. The first few rows actually drew back from its slavering jaws.

No one had any doubts that a creature straight from a nightmare was walking the stage.

Out in the darkness Colin felt the scales drop from his eyes.

How could he have been so blind?

HATE had just been a lure, a minion, he saw that now just as he saw his true mission. Why settle for an acolyte when you can kill the Devil himself?

Out in the darkness Christina gasped.

'Oh God!' she breathed. She didn't need Harry now. The target was identified beyond a shadow of a doubt.

Charlatan had taken the stage.

Chapter 33

Come into my parlour, said the spider to the fly.

It's too easy, Payne thought to himself.
No guards, no alarms, nothing.
He's waiting for me.

Warlord was sitting behind his desk in his apartment overlooking the park. The dying sun cast long shadows through the picture window behind him, draping him in a criss-cross of blackness.
A web.
The door was open.
Come into my parlour.
'Hello, Harry,' he said. 'I've been expecting you.'
Payne moved forward cautiously.
There's a coldness here, his senses told him. A void. Nothingness. Be careful it doesn't swallow you up.
'Is Charlatan my son?' Payne asked without preamble.
The question lay between them like a piece of rotting meat.
'That's classified information, Harry,' Warlord replied. 'Why don't you read my mind and find out for yourself?'
Warlord smiled. It was a small, smug smile. It spoke of secrets shared and promises made.
Payne had been hurting when he made that promise. The pills weren't working; the raw, unfiltered mass of emotions, thoughts and feelings were driving him crazy. Warlord had promised him salvation. The cost at the time seemed small.
'You must never read my mind.' Warlord had said. 'I can help you, Harry, but we must trust each other implicitly, is that clear? I can help you. Never read my mind. I can help you. Never read my mind.'
Such a small price. And so the barriers in Payne's own head had gone up. Conditioning that he'd never questioned.
Until now.
'Is that the only way?' Payne asked.
Warlord nodded. 'The truth is a Pandora's Box, Harry,' he said. 'Are you really sure you want to open it?'
Payne did not speak. He pulled up a chair and sat down.
'So,' Warlord murmured. 'Let battle commence!'

The mind is a room with a thousand locked doors.

To unlock those doors all you need is the key.

Payne approached this door with caution.

Do I really want to know what's behind it?

Warlord was smiling.

He thinks I can't do it!

I promised him.

He's daring me to do it.

He helped me.

He used you.

Warlord was laughing now.

Smug bastard!

He's been like a father to me.

Do you want to know who your son is?

'YES!' Payne screamed and the door flew open.

Warlord wasn't laughing any more. He rocked back in his chair as though hit by an explosion. The muscles in his face were taut, and he gripped the arms of his chair so tightly his knuckles were white.

He's resisting.

I'll break him!

Warlord's body began to shudder. He bit his lip and a thin line of blood trickled from the corner of his mouth and rolled off his chin onto his shirt front.

I'm getting through! I'm getting through!

In his mind's eye, Payne saw a series of cracks appear in Warlord's face. Cracks that became bigger, turning into fissures, letting pieces of his face fall away, revealing another face beneath. That face too began to crack and crumble, showing yet another face beyond. Every face was the same as its predecessor, but younger.

Payne watched the years strip away, until the room began to spin. Suddenly he was somewhere else. He recognised this place. It was his father's house. And there was Warlord, very young, early twenties at most, and there was his father and mother. Until now, Payne had only ever seen his mother in photographs. He realised now that he was seeing her through Warlord's eyes. He never knew she had been quite so beautiful. All three of them were having dinner, talking, laughing.

'She was lovely, wasn't she?' Warlord's voice, a disembodied narrator to his own life's history. 'Your mother, I mean,' he continued. 'I was just a Junior Liaison Officer at the time. Your father was doing some research work for us and we became friends. He was a good man, your father, but weak willed. Your mother, on the other hand, had a will of iron, even though she was physically frail.'

Payne looked down upon her. Her skin was pale, almost translucent, her body thin, her eyes dark-rimmed. She looked so delicate, like a glass sculpture; one breeze and it would shatter beyond repair.

'Your father tried to help her,' Warlord continued. 'In the only way he knew. In his own way he was quite brilliant. I don't think the drugs he gave her actually did her any harm, but they couldn't save her either. Although it might explain why you turned out to be such an unusual specimen, don't you think?'

The scene changed, images blurring, fast forwarding to something different.

I'm just a passenger! Payne realised. I've broken the barrier, but he's still in control!

'So frail of body, but with a will of iron,' Warlord's narration continued. 'That was your mother. She knew exactly what she wanted. And how to get it.'

The images slowed down, came into focus. It was a bedroom, night, two figures locked together, pawing at each other like wild animals.

'No!' Payne screamed. 'I don't want to see this! I don't, I don't!'

'Pandora's Box, Harry.' Warlord chuckled. 'See it all or see nothing.'

The camera in Warlord's mind zoomed in. Payne saw his mother, naked, sweating, her legs wrapped around her lover's buttocks, pushing him deeper and deeper inside her, her face distorted by lust. She was grunting and shouting, repeating the same words over and over again.

'Make a baby, make a baby, make a baby!'

The focus shifted to the man. He was thickset and dark; a coarse layer of black hair covered his chest and shoulders.

'This is wrong!' Payne shouted. 'My father was tall and slim; his hair was so fair it was almost white!'

'Your mother wanted a baby so badly,' Warlord told him, 'she'd do anything to get one. So, when your father proved incapable . . .' He let the words trail off. The camera shifted to the man's face.

Warlord's face.

He's been like a father to me.

He is my father!

'No!' Payne screamed. 'No, no, no, no, no!'

The picture began to spin, dragging him down like a whirlpool, faster and faster, until everything blurred into darkness.

The darkness slowly turned to grey and the lights came up on another scene.

Payne saw himself as a young boy of eleven or twelve. He was walking in the garden with his 'Uncle Joe', the man he would come to know as Warlord.

'Do you play chess?' his uncle asked him.

'No,' the young Payne replied.

'Would you like me to teach you?'

'Yes, please,' he replied eagerly.

'That was how it all began.' Warlord's spectral voice was rich with gloating. 'I was going places by then,' he continued. 'I could see you were special. I knew you could be useful with the right tuition. Your father never forgave you for your mother's death, do you know that? He loved her, you see, and deep inside he blamed you for her dying. I wonder what he'd have thought if he knew he wasn't even the natural father!'

The scene shifted. Scene after scene. Chess game after chess game.

'You were easy to manipulate,' Warlord hissed. 'So young, so eager. Do you remember those conversations we used to have as we played?'

'Yes.' There was a sob in Payne's voice as he replied.

'Sowing the seeds, Harry. Get 'em young and train 'em right, that's what I always say.'

Fast forward.

Snapshots of Harry growing up.

Harry holding Terry Brown's head under water at the baths, until he promised to lend Harry his homework to copy.

Harry bribing two of the fourth form to beat up Eddy Watts because he beat him in the English test.

Harry bribing Jenny Pickford to take her clothes off by buying her an ice cream every day for a week.

'You didn't see those things!' Payne shouted. 'Those are not your memories!'

'But you told me about them, Harry,' Warlord replied. 'Don't you remember? When we played chess you told me all your secrets. You liked the feeling of power even then, didn't you, Harry? If people didn't do what you wanted, you found a way to make them, or else you made them pay. You learned well, Harry. Who knows, you may have been just a common little thug if the headaches hadn't started.'

Fast forward.

Harry as a teenager. The screaming fits, the tantrums.

'You thought you were losing your mind,' Warlord said. 'Instead, you were simply gaining access to other people's! You didn't know it at the time. Neither did I, not for sure, and your father had no idea whatsoever. So he tried to come up with a chemical solution to your problem without really knowing its real nature! For an intelligent man he could really be so foolish at times. Give him his due, it worked, after a fashion, but it wasn't enough. Our solution was better, wasn't it, Harry?'

Focus on Harry and Uncle Joe.

'Let's play a game,' Uncle Joe said.

'What kind of game?' Harry replied, truculent and surly.

'Let's pretend you're a spy. You have to come up with an entirely new identity for yourself, and I have to quiz you to see if I can trick you into making mistakes. Do you like the sound of that?'

'It sounds stupid!'

'Try it anyway. You might get to like it.'

At first the questions were easy.

What's your name?

What's your favourite colour?

Where do you live?

Gradually they became more complex. The boy that had been Harry Payne had to concentrate more and more to keep up. The more he concentrated, the more the headaches and the voices were kept at bay, until finally his other identity was so ingrained he had trouble remembering who he really was.

'It was a strange and wonderful metamorphosis,' Warlord informed him. 'I knew by then what potential you really had. All that was left were the field trials.'

Fast forward.

Harry with Roger.

Harry with Laura.

Harry with Debbie.

'Such a clever boy,' Warlord intoned smugly. 'Three separate lives in addition to your own. What a clever little schizophrenic you were becoming. Naturally, your father didn't approve. By this time it was difficult to keep our little secret under wraps. We had a falling out, he and I, but I wasn't worried. I knew you would come to me of your own accord. I just didn't know in what way!'

Fast forward.

Harry and his father. The last time he had seen him alive. They were rowing. The words were indistinct, distorted. His father clutched his chest and keeled over. Fade to black.

'I really do think, Harry,' Warlord said, 'that you may actually have killed him without realising it. But what you did next you were very much aware of, weren't you, Harry?'

Fast forward.

'With your father gone, you had no one to give you any more pills, did you, Harry? I could have helped, but I was out of the country at the time. I only got back right at the very end. Perhaps it was fate. It was certainly those events that brought your power into full bloom. I look upon these as your graduation photos, Harry.'

He watched them again in every detail. Smelt the blood, felt the flesh give as he plunged the knife in, felt the glorious rush of emotion that was released with every thrust. He felt no remorse. He'd lived with these memories every day of his adult life. These and more. Oh, these were the first, but he'd done far worse since. There was only one difference.

For the first three, he was clinically insane, of that he was sure, but the others? He was not only sane, he was acting under orders. Uncle Joe's orders. Uncle Joe, who had orchestrated this bloodbath right from the start. So, who's the real monster here, Uncle? You or me?

Fast forward.

Warlord's face, concerned, but calm.

'I can help you, but we have to trust each other implicitly. You must never read my mind. Do you agree?'

'Yes.'

'Good. Just sign everything over to me, Harry, and I'll take care of you.'

'This is where we came in, Harry.'

'Not quite.'

'Ah, yes. Who's that knocking at my door?'

Fast forward.

Sandy. The scene plays in silence. Warlord laughs.

He's enjoying this!

'She was just a little tramp, Harry. You didn't need her. But she claimed to be carrying your baby! I didn't know if it was true or not, but I couldn't take the chance. I was going to have her killed. It would have been easy to arrange. And then I thought of the possibilities. What if she really was carrying your child? What if he turned out just like you? So I gave her money instead. Enough to keep her mouth shut. I was careless, I admit it. I should have eliminated her as soon as the child was born, but I was in a good mood. The little tyke was obviously going to be a real asset to me.'

'So you started all over again?'

'Right from scratch. But he wasn't anywhere near as good a student as you. His powers were quite remarkable, but his mind was shit. Nothing worked. So I had to use you, didn't I, Harry? What else could I do?'

Show's over.

A sudden elevator lurch and reality swam back into view.

Warlord sagged forward in his chair; his face was scarlet and drenched in sweat. Large wet patches stained his crisp white shirt. He was panting, gasping for breath, his muscles locked painfully from the strain of keeping control.

By contrast Payne was pale, almost white, his body trembled and he breathed rapidly through his nose, on the verge of hyperventilating.

Warlord slowly raised his head.

'Did you see enough, Harry?' he asked.

'I am your son!' The anguish in his voice turned it raw and ragged. 'And you turned me into this!'

'And you loved it, Harry. I could see it in you right from the start.'

'You saw what you wanted to see. A reflection of yourself.'

'I made you the best, Harry.'

'You made me a monster!'

'Hardly. But I did make you more than a man.'

'And now you want me to do the same to my son, your own grandson?'

'Why not? Carry on the family tradition. What do you say?'

'Go to hell!'

'I'm sorry you feel that way, Harry.'

The gun appeared in his hand as if by magic.

'I really can't let you go, Harry, you know that, don't you?'

Payne had time for one fleeting thought.

He had it in his lap all this time, and I never sensed a thing!

Then there was a dull explosion, a short burst of flame and Payne fell to the floor.

Chapter 34

Sonia screamed and clutched her side.

Doubling over, she fell forward, only the crush of bodies keeping her upright.

Christina grabbed her under the arms and pulled her aside.

'I knew you were sick!' Christina shouted above the noise.

Sonia's only reply was a groan.

Muttering a curse under her breath, Christina hauled Sonia to her feet and bulled her way through the crowd.

The entrance hall was cooler, the noise muffled by heavy swing doors.

Christina stumbled and nearly fell. She leant against the wall for support and lowered Sonia to a sitting position on the floor.

A bouncer moved from his position at the door, coming in their direction.

'She okay?' he asked.

'Just fainted, that's all,' Christina replied. 'She'll be fine in a minute. Really.'

'If she's gonna spew,' he said, 'get her into the bog first, okay?'

Christina nodded. 'Fine,' she agreed. His duty done, the bouncer moved back to his post.

Christina leaned close to Sonia's face and hissed, 'What the hell's the matter with you?'

'Payne,' Sonia mumbled, 'Payne.'

'Where?' Christina asked, misunderstanding. 'Is it your ribs, your kidneys, what?'

Sonia shook her head. 'No,' she muttered. 'It's Harry!'

'Harry? What about him?

'He's hurt. Bad. I can feel his pain!' Sonia held a shaking hand up to her face, as though expecting to see it covered with blood.

'Christ Almighty!' Christina muttered. 'Will you be okay for a while?' she asked. 'I have to go back inside.'

Sonia nodded. 'Go,' she said. 'I just need to rest, that's all.' She closed her eyes and her head fell forward onto her chest.

Christina checked her pulse. It was weak, but steady. She stood up.

'My friend just needs to rest for a while,' she told the bouncer, who was still eyeing them suspiciously. 'Can I leave her here while I go back inside?'

Christina didn't wait for an answer. 'Thanks,' she called over her shoulder, as she pushed her way back through the double doors.

Don't believe what you see in movies.

When you get shot, you can't just wrap a handkerchief around it and carry on as if nothing has happened.

The body goes into shock, it closes down and even a minor wound can incapacitate.

Payne had a hole through his left side. He was lying on his back, his body twitching spasmodically.

Warlord levered himself shakily from his seat.

'Why couldn't you just have followed orders?' Warlord asked.

He didn't expect an answer. He shuffled forward, his body sluggish and unresponsive. He sighted down the barrel of the gun. His finger tightened on the trigger.

The pain took him like a hammer blow in the left side of his chest. His knees buckled and he twisted sideways, clutching the desk for support. The gun fell from nerveless fingers.

Payne opened his eyes.

'No!' Warlord whimpered. 'No!'

Payne rolled slowly onto his uninjured side and hauled himself up to a sitting position.

'You underestimate me!' he spat.

Warlord felt the pressure begin to build inside his skull.

Got to get away! Got to get away! The message flashed in Warlord's skull like a neon sign. He swayed and staggered, but his legs refused to function. He felt the blood begin to flow from his ears and nose. He took one step, then another, before falling flat on his face.

He was dead before he hit the floor.

How does he do that?

Cathy was fainting from the heat, the crush of bodies and the excitement. He was close enough to touch and she still couldn't see how he did that!

He began as a lizard man, crawling from the pit, his skin covered in scales, his eyes bulbous with a vertical pupil, his tongue at least a foot long and forked. He slithered on his belly, hands and feet webbed and clawed. The crowd went wild as he dragged himself upright on the microphone stand and started to sing 'Voices From The Other Side'. It was the track that Lenny Pepper had been playing all week, and it was so cool it sent shivers down Cathy's spine.

But that was just the start.

The second number was called 'Shed My Skin', and that's exactly what he did! Right up there, in front of everyone, his skin just cracked wide open, the scales fading away, talons contracting, eyes changing to deepest blue, and he howled, and the wolf was born! Lean and hairy, with pointed ears, strutting and pouting like Jagger after a bad case of lycanthropy!

And his voice!

One second it was Jagger, then Bowie, then Presley, then back to Jagger again! The whole building shook with the vibrations as the crowd stamped and screamed their approval.

There was no break between numbers; they just steamed on like a runaway train.

'This one is called "Dance With The Devil"!' he told them.

He stuck his face into the spotlight and horns began to grow from his forehead!

'Who wants to dance with the Devil?' he screamed at them.

Nearly a thousand voices replied, 'Me, me, me, take me!'

He strutted across the front of the stage, teasing, slapping at outstretched hands. Then he leapt forward, his choice made, and Cathy felt herself being pulled over the footlights!

It was like stepping into a sauna.

Christina's clothes were plastered to her body. She pushed her way to the side wall and began to make her way to the front of the hall. Get backstage, catch him when he comes off, straight to the car and away before anyone realises what's going on.

Nice plan, she told herself sarcastically, but it was the only one she had.

Damn you, Harry Payne, she thought, damn you to hell!

Dancing with the Devil!

Oh God, I'm a star!

The lights, the heat, the adrenalin rush made Cathy feel like she was flying.

Oh God, this is fantastic!

The crowd were clapping and cheering.

They're cheering me!

Cathy turned to the audience, her audience, reached down and pulled her tee-shirt over her head. She had nothing on underneath and the crowd roared their approval.

Cathy laughed and threw her shirt into the crowd, watching it get ripped to shreds.

Then Darth moved in behind her, running his hands up and down her body.

Oh God, I'm going to die, this is so good!

Out of the corner of her eye she saw a scuffle break out at the side of the stage.

Christina was almost there.

Almost at the side door that led backstage. Charlatan was groping some half-naked piece of jailbait.

Enjoy it while you can, Charlie, she thought grimly, enjoy it while you can!

The crowd around her ebbed and flowed like waves crashing against the shore. Christina fought against it, trying to keep a straight course, but forced to take detours, craning her neck above the human sea every now and then to chart her progress.

And then it changed. The pattern of movement altered, ripples spreading out from the far side of the room. People turned, pushing towards the source of the disturbance. Christina had to jump to see clearly. She saw a figure in a bulky anorak pull loose from clutching hands and scramble onto the stage.

In his hand he held a gun.

Oh Christ! It's Colin. And he's got a gun!

Cathy stopped dancing and stared aghast at the dishevelled figure as he brought the gun up and pointed it straight at her.

'In the name of God!' he screamed, 'let her go!'

The band stopped playing. The whole world went unnaturally quiet and began to move in slow motion.

Cathy turned to run.

Darth began to move forward and to the right.

Someone in the crowd lashed out at Colin's legs, bringing him to his knees.

The gun went off.

A hole appeared in Cathy's back. Her chest exploded and she skidded across the stage on her face.

With the gunshot came a tidal surge of bodies, tripping and crushing each other in their haste, some to get away, some to get closer to the centre of attention.

Christina saw an opening and plunged forward. Almost falling up the steps that led to the stage, she cannoned into the wall, then righted herself.

Colin had kicked free of the clutching hands that had dragged him down. Desperately he tried to bring the gun up once more, but Darth was upon him before he could even stand up.

Darth grabbed Colin by the collar and hauled him clear off the ground. Colin made a choked, gurgling sound and dropped his gun. Darth pulled him so close that Colin could feel his spittle spray his cheeks as he roared at him:

'DO YOU PLAY CHESS?'

The microphones were still open and the Avalon Radio listeners heard his question loud and clear.

Christina groaned inwardly and reached under her jacket for her own gun.

As she did so, the crowd began to chant.

'Kill him! Kill him! Kill him!'

Darth began to shake the helpless Colin like a rag doll, making his body flop and jerk, like a sack of loose bones.

'Charlatan!' Christina screamed at the top of her lungs. 'Charlatan, put him down! Now!'

Even above the chant of the crowd, Christina heard the sickening snap as Colin's neck broke like a twig.

Christina shut her eyes tight, tears squeezing from beneath her closed lids.

Oh Jesus! she thought. How could it all go so wrong?

When she opened her eyes, Charlatan was moving slowly towards her, Colin's corpse a forgotten bundle of rags on the floor.

The crowd, lost in its chant, noticed her for the first time. She could feel their bloodlust turn towards her like a wave of heat from a furnace.

Christina had assumed the classic shooting stance, legs spread wide for balance, arms straight out, left hand gripping right wrist to steady the aim.

'Don't make me do it, Charlie!' she pleaded. 'Don't make me do it!'

He ignored her, dancing forward, with a red light in his eyes.

'Do you want to play, too?' he asked. 'Do you want to play chess?'

Charlatan sprang forward, hands reaching for Christina's throat.

She pulled the trigger.

Christina felt the force of the explosion, saw Charlatan twist in mid-air, the force of his lunge carrying him into her, knocking the breath from her body. Something hot and wet sprayed her chest and neck.

Blood, she thought, his blood! Then she was falling, the hard edges of the stairs catching her back and sides. The gun jarred from her hand.

Winded, dazed, Christina heard rather than saw the crowd surge in around her, a deafening scream of primal rage.

Rough hands pulled her to her feet, slammed her against the wall. She saw faces, hundreds of them, all twisted, not human, no longer individuals, just part of some huge primitive creature craving blood.

Her blood.

Someone kneed her in the stomach and she fell forward. A bottle exploded against her temple and she felt the jagged edge rip a hole in her cheek. As she crouched, gagging and dizzy, the boots started flying. The first one took her in the face, breaking her nose, snapping her head back in a plume of scarlet. The rest landed on her sides and legs. She felt a rib pop.

Hands reached in, ripping at her clothes, clawing skin in the process. They punched and ripped and punched some more. Christina tried to shield herself with her arms, but they were viciously wrenched aside and back. She screamed as her shoulder dislocated, and still they punched and tore at her.

Finally, they hoisted her onto their shoulders, naked and bloody, and threw her into the crowd. Hands reached up to catch her, eager for their piece of the action. Christina was unconscious before they caught her.

By the time they passed her on a second time, she was dead.

On stage, Molly cradled Charlie's head in her arms, trying to stop the flow of blood with her hands, crying and screaming all at the same time.

'Get an ambulance!' she shouted. 'For God's sake get an ambulance!' Her voice was lost in the fury and destruction.

Molly held him close and watched him change, the Darth Presley wolfman giving way to the soft, gentle features she loved.

'Hold on, Charlie,' she whispered. 'Please, hold on!'

Charlie looked up at her with eyes that had lost their fire. He coughed and a bubble of blood burst from his lips. Molly wiped the crimson spill away with her hand.

'It was the Bad Man,' Charlie whispered. 'He was inside me all along!' There was a note of childlike wonder in his voice. He coughed again and his whole body shook. Molly held him tight until the tremor had passed.

'It's all right now,' he said. 'He's gone now, he's not inside me any more. I'm free!'

'I love you, Charlie!' Molly almost shouted, her tears mingling with the blood streaked across his face.

With trembling fingers, Charlie reached up to touch her cheek.

'And ... I ... love ... you ... too,' he said.

The last word was a long drawn-out sigh. His eyes closed and his head fell back.

Chapter 35

Bannerman wandered disconsolately from one body bag to another.
Four of them.
Jesus Christ, it was a massacre!
He stopped and unzipped one of the bags enough to see the face.
It was smooth and unblemished, young and innocent, peaceful in death.
There were too many unanswered questions.
Serial killers.
Mass hysteria.
Bannerman shook his head.
'I'm getting too old for this!' he said out loud.
The case would no doubt be formally closed, but it wouldn't be forgotten.
Not this time.
Not by Bannerman.
Bannerman and elephants never forget.

Chapter 36

No one attended the funeral.

It was an unmarked grave in a lonely corner of the cemetery.

From a small rise a young woman watched the last clod of earth laid and saw the gravediggers depart. She stood for a while, just looking, then she turned and walked briskly out of the cemetery to where her companion was waiting in the car.

'It's quite a nice spot, really,' she said. 'Secluded and peaceful. Are you sure you don't want to see it?'

Payne shook his head. 'You saw it,' he replied. 'That's good enough.'

Since the shooting his rapport with Sonia had increased to the extent that he could now see through her eyes and she through his. He seemed content to depend on her both physically and mentally, at least until he healed properly.

'It's not far,' she said. 'I could help you.'

'No,' he replied. There was no anger in his voice as there once would have been. He just sounded so very tired. Tired and empty.

Sonia started the engine.

'Where are we going?' she asked.

'Anywhere,' he said. 'It doesn't matter any more.'

Chapter 37

The bus station was busy.

Molly scanned the crowd, looking for familiar faces.

She saw none.

That was good. She didn't like tearful goodbyes. Although, she had to admit, anyone seeing her now would be hard put to recognise her.

Her blonde hair had been cropped short and allowed to revert to its natural, mousy colour. She disguised her figure by wearing extra-large sweaters and baggy overalls. She carried the rest of her worldly goods in a holdall.

The coach was on time for once. Molly boarded with half a dozen others, thankful to have a seat to herself for at least part of the journey. The last thing she wanted was to have to make polite conversation. She had too much to think about.

As the coach pulled out, Molly smiled down at the way her hands were clasped protectively around her stomach.

'It's just you and me now,' she whispered. 'Just you and me and a whole new life.'

The foetus growing inside her was too small to show yet, let alone hear her, but somehow she felt he understood. Just as she knew it would be a boy.

A boy just like his father.

Special.